Effortless
Tears

Effortless Tears

Alexander Kanengoni

Baobab Books
1993

Published by Baobab Books, P.O. Box 567, Harare
A division of Academic Books (Pvt) Ltd, Harare, 1993

Cover design: Paul Wade, Inkspots

Illustrations: Paul Wade, Inkspots

Typeset by: Baobab Books (Pvt) Ltd

Printed by: Mazongororo Paper Converters (Pvt) Ltd

ISBN 0-908311-61-3

Alexander Kanengoni, author of *Vicious Circle*, was born in Chivu in 1951. He went to school at Marymount Mission and continued his studies at Kutama College, St Paul's Teacher Training College and the University of Zimbabwe where he majored in English.

For seven years, he fought with the nationalist guerrillas. At independence he joined the Ministry of Education and Culture. He is currently head of Television Services with the Zimbabwe Broadcasting Corporation.

Contents

Glossary

Amai	–	Mrs, mother
Baba	–	Mr
baba	–	father
Baba VaTinashe	–	father of Tinashe
Castle	–	light beer
hosho	–	rattle
kachasu	–	home-brewed beer made from maize or millet, fruit, yeast, etc
Lion	–	light beer
Mai	–	Mrs
mbira	–	thumb piano
mudhara	–	old man
mujibha	–	scouts; messengers; look-outs. Young men and boys who acted for the freedom fighters
mukuwasha	–	son-in-law; loosely used to mean brother/friend
n'anga	–	healer; herbalist; quack
pamberi	–	forward
Selous Scouts	–	notorious special unit of the Rhodesian army formed in November 1973
shamwari	–	friend
Va	–	Mr, father

Glossary

Amai	–	Mrs, mother
Baba	–	Mr
baba	–	father
Baba VaTinashe	–	father of Tinashe
Castle	–	light beer
hosho	–	rattle
kachasu	–	home-brewed beer made from maize or millet, fruit, yeast, etc
Lion	–	light beer
Mai	–	Mrs
mbira	–	thumb piano
mudhara	–	old man
mujibha	–	scouts; messengers; look-outs. Young men and boys who acted for the freedom fighters
mukuwasha	–	son-in-law; loosely used to mean brother/friend
n'anga	–	healer; herbalist; quack
pamberi	–	forward
Selous Scouts	–	notorious special unit of the Rhodesian army formed in November 1973
shamwari	–	friend
Va	–	Mr, father

Kangaire (1960)

The priest bowed and kissed the makeshift altar. He genuflected and faced the thin congregation. With his face raised piously heavenwards, he spread out his arms: "May the Almighty God bless you and keep you," he said making the sign of the cross. "In the name of the Father, Son and Holy Ghost."

"Amen," chorused the congregation. They stood up and uneasily flexed their cramped muscles. The men hitched up their khaki trousers and straightened their cheap ties and slouch hats. The women adjusted and brushed the seats of their dresses and hushed to silence the restless babies on their backs. All of them mopped their sweating faces and picked up their Bibles and hymn books. The service was over.

A woman with a high, wiry voice struck up the lead of an alms-giving song. Everyone took it up. A small boy in a khaki shirt and shorts moved from row to row with a cup. Pennies, tickeys[1] and an occasional sixpence jingled into

[1] Small silver coin: threepence.

1

the cup. Meanwhile the priest, Father Hanz, took off his holy garments. He was tall and middle-aged with strong features. A server folded the garments neatly and packed them into the priest's travelling bag.

The heat was unbearable. The sun travelled the cloudless sky with uncompromising abandon. The arid countryside was still and desolate. Its huge *musasa* and *mupfuti* trees were silent and leafless. No birds fluttered among their naked branches. The atmosphere smelt of ash. The long grass that had once clothed the countryside had been burnt at the beginning of the dry season by villagers, who .lived on the edges of the purchase area[2], prior to setting out on their clandestine hunting expeditions. But the steady flow of new farmers on to the land was slowly discouraging this practice.

The singing voices of the congregants under the *musasa* tree echoed across the lethargic afternoon. The song came to an end when the small boy carried the barely full cup of coins to the half-dismantled altar. Someone from the congregation introduced another tune that told of a time of plenty. The woman with the wiry voice tiptoed over to a plump communicant and whispered something into her ear. The plump woman tilted her head attentively and nodded. She adjusted the baby on her back and walked over to consult two other women. The three of them lit a fire beyond the circle of worshippers and began to prepare the priest's food. They had brought a hen, eggs and some mealie-meal from their homes for this purpose. It was something they did every month.

The priest carried his bag to his motor-bike. Behind him the hymn died away. The small congregation broke up and people shook hands and began enquiring about each other's health and discussed the latest arrivals.

The priest walked over from his motor-bike. He beamed as he shook hands with people. He spoke in halting Shona. Everyone laughed. "I don't think I will ever be able to speak Shona. In Nyasaland, I was never able to speak

---

[2] An area within the Tribal Trust Land set apart for sale to African farmers of proven experience.

Chewa and in Northern Rhodesia I could not speak Nyanja. And now I'm trying Shona and I mix the words of all three languages," he lamented.

"But you already know how to speak Shona, *Baba*," said the woman with the wiry voice.

"You are flattering me."

"No. You are coming up all right." There was laughter.

The place never changed, nor did the sequence of conversation. The people only varied in so far as new faces occasionally added to their thin numbers. The place was everybody's: a fairly large chunk of empty land cut out between the farms. Such empty land was called Crown Land. It was envisaged that public amenities such as schools, churches, shops and dams for people on the surrounding farms would be built one day. But so far, they remained dry plans held in an office somewhere. The cry from the new farmers was for water. There was no water and no reservoirs and it worried them. Daily they drove their dying animals miles to the few dams that did exist. Life was hard. The land was hard.

An old man snapped the fingers of his raised hand. Father Hanz sat on a fallen tree trunk in front of the people. One of his servers stood by to translate. The men sat on stones and tree stumps and the women cross-legged on the ground. In the sky overhead, the October sun beat down on them.

One old man stood up. "We could build a small church but what we need most is water. For how long will we survive without a dam? Our beasts are weary and many die on the long distances they have to travel for water."

"I am sorry but I have to tell you once again that there is nothing that I can do about this. I am only a priest."

"But you could always bring it to their attention next time you see them," someone appealed.

The priest shook his head in desperation. "I report to my own superiors. I don't even know the District Commissioner in this area."

3

"We make regular representations to him but all we get are promises. We are tired of his promises. We bought these small farms just as the whites did in the adjacent Mutungagore area! They have water; we don't. Why did they open up this area without sufficient facilities? We are tired."

"Can't you tell your superiors to put pressure on the DC? These problems get into the way of everything, even your work," the woman with the wiry voice said. "I think the only way to make the DC act is to force him to do something." Everyone looked at her sceptically.

"This year is already over and our children are at home with us. Next year will be just as bleak because there still won't be any school. What should we do?" someone asked.

The priest shrugged his shoulders helplessly: the sequence of conversation was always the same. They always resulted in a fruitless discussion of the general problems of the area. Father Hanz was not only their parish priest, he was also their leader. But there was nothing he could do, or nothing he thought he could do.

Not far away from the huge *musasa* tree there was a river. It was dry. The river-bed was sandy and full of stones. It cut a deep dry path through the small farms.

During the dry season the river possessed an eerie, naked emptiness. It was a lifeless giant that with the first rains would become a menacing presence. Along its eroded banks reeds would grow green and tall, birds would dart from the trees to the water, fish would also swim up its course from the Ruya River only to get stranded upstream as the water unpredictably dried up. For a long time the river had no name. Then people gave it one – someone's off-hand suggestion – Kangaire. And so, it became known as Kangaire, a name that did not mean anything.

Some two or so hours later, only a few people still remained. The rest had drifted back to their homes. Father Hanz stood by his motor-bike ready for the return journey to Marymount Mission. The woman with the wiry voice edged closer to him, pushing her two children in front of her.

"Please, *Baba*, give my son and daughter each a blessing," she asked.

"By all means, Mai Choto."

He patted the boy on the shoulder. "How old are they?"

"The boy is nine and the girl is six."

"Nine and six! So many years?" He swept the girl into his arms. She began chewing her thumb.

"Get that thumb out of your mouth!" the mother snapped at her.

"Big girls don't chew thumbs, they chew pens," the priest said.

"What are their names?" he asked.

"Brian and Mercy."

"What does your name mean?" he asked the boy.

The boy began to draw patterns on the ground with his sandal. "I don't know," he said.

"What then do you know?" the priest challenged.

The boy looked up at him defiantly. "Many things," he said imperiously.

"What then are your years added to your sister's?"

"Just that! . . . Fifteen."

"And a bright one too!" the priest said turning to the mother.

"He is bright but what can he do without going to school?"

"Why don't you send him to one now?"

"Now? Where?"

"Marymount. What did you say his name was?"

"Brian," the little boy answered for himself. The priest cast him an envious glance as he fumbled for his notebook.

"I've got my boy too," said the plump woman.

"And mine too," said another woman.

"Okay. Okay," said the priest trying to halt the avalanche of voices. "We will talk about it next time I come here."

He hastily straddled his motor-bike and kicked the starter motor. The machine spluttered into life. The deafening sound rang across the drowsy afternoon, infinitely echoing and making the earth tremble. He fastened his crash-helmet, thrust the machine into gear and the monster lurched away. The few remaining people anxiously waved him goodbye and the priest waved back.

The sequence of events had been the same; it was always the same, but there was nothing that he could do about it and he felt low in spirit. Was he supposed to climb the highest mountain without anyone to help him? In his mind, ideas were already forming. What was needed most was water, then a school. If only he could get these two things moving, the rest would come later.

A few people stood staring after the receding motor-bike as the noise died away in the distance. They bade each other goodbye and silently walked back to their homes. Only Brian still remembered that the priest had forgotten to give them the blessing his mother had requested.

There was a river. Its banks were steep and deep. During the dry season the river was dry and naked with nothing to suggest that it might one day fill with water. For some obscure reason, people called it Kangaire, a name without meaning or connotation. In time, the name came to designate an empty piece of land incomprehensibly given to the Crown thousands of miles away in Britain: a piece of dry land under whose huge *musasa* and *mupfuti* trees different religious groups gathered to conduct their Sunday services.

There was a river. It wound its way upstream from the Crown Land for some four or five files to its source – a small plain wedged between two ridges. Cutting across this plain was a road with steep sides and numerous potholes, deteriorating from disuse. Very few cars and only a single bus travelled it once a week. To the east, the road crawled to Marymount Mission some sixty miles away. Branching from out of the road in the narrow valley was an almost invisible path. This gloomy path was the only way to Kangaire.

Kangaire Revisited (1977)

The priest, Father Hanz, bowed and kissed the makeshift altar. He genuflected and tripped over the hem of his ankle-length gown. He staggered. His dull eyes flickered for an instant. He raised his head and his lips moved silently. "May the Almighty God bless you," he said at last. "Father, Son and Holy Spirit." The congregation's "Amen" was drowned in the jarring reverberations of helicopters as they came in to land at the military base on the other side of the dam. Everyone knelt anxiously, their attention focused on the nightmare that so often accompanied the sound. Most peered furtively through the open double doors. They saw nothing. Others rubbed the beads of perspiration collecting on their foreheads and stared at the huge cross hanging above the altar. The air reeked with desperation.

After the noise had died away the priest repeated the blessing. The "Amen" from the people was a hollow, emotionless whisper.

Someone from the congregation, a man, began an alms-giving song. Sister Tracy, VaGwara's daughter from the neighbourhood, tiptoed down the aisle with an alms plate. The song wound its way wearily round the building with Mai Choto miraculously rescuing it at every corner. With her hymn book held firmly before her, her wiry voice rose high above everyone else's. Sister Tracy returned the empty plate to the altar. Times were difficult.

The priest and his two servers walked slowly down the aisle to the chapel at the rear of the church. Behind them, the song fell like the sound of a herdboy's worn-out whip. Only Mai Choto's wiry voice was audible from outside.

The early morning sun beat down upon the tense countryside making the corrugated roofing sheets of Kangaire Mission shimmer. But sadly, most of the buildings lay abandoned and empty. They stood desolate with their doors ripped out. Inside, the desks and tables remained but because no one cared for them, they were rotting and would soon disappear. The walls bore glaring cracks and the coming rains would further destroy the remaining structures. What were once the teachers' houses had had their roofs blown away by the wind. All that remained of the school were the scars of dashed hope. It had been closed for over a year due to the long guerrilla war.

Since 1960, a lot of things had happened and nothing stood in the people's minds but the war: a bitter, swift, ruthless war. Nearly everyone had heard of different wars but few had taken part in one. Here and there on an isolated farm, some elderly man would boast that he had fought for the Crown against Hitler but they all admitted that that experience was nothing like this. The very, very old like Sekuru Maruta would also boast about their kind of war: the conflict at the end of the last century against the occupying forces of the white man. But compared to this war, it seemed to have been mere child's play. They were now witnessing a strange kind of war in which they, the unarmed, played the major role.

The school had been closed because the authorities suspected that it was being used to harbour guerrillas. The domestic science, driving and mechanics' workshops had also been closed down. There had also been a clinic. It had closed. The daily bus service to Salisbury had long been suspended. The people lived in a cordoned off area without either services from, or communication with, the outside world. The people were fighting a war without dividing lines and with nothing to suggest it was taking place except the everyday sight of the fighter bombers, helicopters, armoured troop carriers and the occasional encounter with a group of AK-carrying guerrillas. And of course the nightmare of a military vehicle detonating a land mine somewhere near their homes or a clash between the guerrillas and the security forces in the vicinity.

The alms-giving song tottered before it finally died away. The service was over. The thin congregation trooped out. The people stood in clumsy groups anxiously glancing at the military camp across the school football field. There were no young men or women around. They had all fled to the congested safety of the cities. Others like Brian and his sister Mercy had fled into the wilderness to join the liberation forces.

After the service people did not talk for long. Their hushed discussion about life and war was disrupted by the sound of an approaching military Land-Rover. They quickly broke up and shuffled away to the permanent uncertainty of their homes. Even as they did this, they all rummaged uneasily for their identity documents in their pockets. They also worried about the rumour that they were soon to be herded into protected villages like cattle. If the soldiers did that, they mused, well there was nothing anyone could do about it. The atmosphere was taut with a brittle fear.

As Father Hanz shuffled towards his office, he met Mai Choto. She was thin and battered and she walked with a perpetual limp. He felt a sudden impulse to call out and reassure her but he restrained himself. He remembered the letter. He had found it under his door the previous day. It was from Brian, her son, who had fled from the university where he had been doing a degree in economics. It seemed he had now re-surfaced with the guerrillas. How quickly the priest had committed some of the lines to memory.

"We have committed ourselves to the politics of self-installation. We have opted for war as a last resort to bring peace. The only way to arrive at justice is through blood. All around me is revolution and it is unfortunately all that I can talk about."

Father Hanz could almost feel the physical presence of the small boy nearly two decades ago in that letter. Brian. At that time Kangaire had been just a barren chunk of land. He shuffled faster towards his office. His lips dropped into a sad smile as he looked at the approaching military Land-Rover. He was certain Kangaire would very soon come full circle. And then tears for something that he did not understand, started welling up in his old eyes.

There was a river. Its banks were hard and steep. During the dry season, the river was dry and naked. For some obscure reason, the people called it Kangaire, a name without meaning or connotation. In time, the name came to signify more. It came to mean that particular dry and empty piece of land under whose *musasa* and *mupfuti* trees different religious groups gathered to conduct their Sunday services.

The Rift

Farai hitched up his trousers. As always on such occasions, he was worried. Should he meet the old man, his father, in the present or in the past? Lately, he had taught himself to let the old man set the time and the occasion.

The old man sat on his leopard-skin mat, feeding wood into the dying fire. His spear was stuck in the ground beside him. His ox-hide shield was also beside him. So too was his *mbira*, his calabash, the percussion instruments, the earthen pitcher with its ladle and, of course, his axe. The time and the occasion had been set for a hunting expedition.

The old man looked at his son disapprovingly. Anger flickered in his dull eyes. . . the boy was naked! He asked why the boy should come empty-handed, without a trace of his manhood. It was not a question, it was an accusation. The son shrugged his shoulders and sat down, his mind groping for something he could never obtain. Yes, he had been given a spear, a shield and percussion instruments. They were there to push him past the threshold into manhood.

The old man saw himself and his dead father in his son. Why then should his son stand naked? But he knew that the boy would not answer. He took his own percussion instruments and handed them to his son. He then took his *mbira* and set them in the calabash. He hit the glittering *mbira* keys and the boy shook the *hosho*. It was their way, disentangling the present. They were searching for a way to begin.

The song swirled out of the smouldering smoke. It was *Nyamaropa*, a hunters' song, as they set out for the dark and eerie forests. It told of the promises of the mountains and the rivers, unfolding their mysteries and myths. The old man quickly felt the euphoria of the song, but deep inside his heart he knew that his son would never see the stamping feet and the flapping animal skins as men and women lost themselves in the song. He also knew that the boy would never hear the whining of excited dogs raring to race through the forests. He would never see the brandishing spears: neither would he ever hear the long, drawn-out ululations of the women.

The old man heard and saw these things and he wanted his son to see and hear them as he did. In particular he wanted him to see the younger men, seemingly careless but alert, girding their loins and brandishing their spears as they out-leapt the older men, the younger women entranced, their breasts quivering with their feelings for the younger men, the old man wanted his son to see these things but he knew the boy would never see them. His son's reaction was the first hurdle, his fulfilment as elusive as the clouds in an endless drought.

The music rallied. Along the dark horizon, storm clouds gathered. The old man looked up into the sky for more time, around him at dying time and into himself at lost time. The son looked up into the sky at ambling time, around him at regenerating time and into himself at discovered time. Their eyes met and locked. Pain. Farai winced and swung the *hosho* more wildly. The old man hit the keys of his *mbira* just as wildly.

He chuckled. The music throbbed. The rains came. The hunters move out of the kraal. The village recedes behind them. The mountains swirl and rise from behind the mist like some awakening giants. . . the old man was now unfolding the saga. It was the same old story reverberating through the generations. It was about the tragedy of the land, its value shrinking with time. And the land slouching miserably on. Here, the old man struck a formidable parallel: the hunters went out but came back. Preceding generations initiated succeeding generations into the myths of the veld. But today's youth go out alone and unattended. They walk out of their homes with their backs stiff, armed only with the shadow of the white man's promise. They go with their sense of belonging, feeling guilty at having been born rural. They bury their past behind the first corner they take. They don't bring back anything because they never come back. They go to explore the abyss. Somewhere on the way, they crash headlong into obstacles and die. Those who are lucky realize that the land is yesterday, today and tomorrow. They trudge back holding together the small pieces of their dashed dreams. They find the land barren and dry, miserably slouching on.

The music slumped into a groove that it had moulded for itself. There, *Nyamaropa* would die. The message had been delivered. What the old man wanted was an assurance that would guarantee its continuity. Everyone in his lineage measured the success of his life that way. That was how he wanted his son to measure the fulfilment of his life.

There was hardly a moment to pause as out of the gulley where *Nyamaropa* was hunted down another tune began – *Nhemamusasa,* another hunting song. The hunters have frightened away the dangerous prey and it is dark. They are tired and rest for the night. The old man hit his *mbira* harder. His son accompanied him with the whirring *hosho*. The calabash trebled the sound which hung over the evening's stillness.

The old man looked at his son, past him and back again into his own mind. He could see them very easily, the hunters spread out and sleeping. There too were the glowing embers of dying fires. He also saw the young men on guard, as dark as the trees against which they were leaning. He saw all this through his son. His heart ached. He knew his son would never see these things.

The music veered into a new crescendo. Its beat doubled and redoubled. They all could hear the disturbing fury of the thickening storm. Then it closed in and the boy replied: "Yes, father, the land is everything. The land is life. The land is our identity. But where is the land? There is no land. There is no life."

The old man's wrinkled face relaxed. In his son's eyes, he began to see the broken pieces of his own dreams. He drew his lips back into a reproachful but forgiving smile. Together they had never gone this far before.

The son continued. "When we still had the land, we treasured it. We subjected it to our instincts which were gradually shaped by the flying dust churned by the shuffling feet of passing generations. We trod a path that led somewhere. The movement was immense, as formidable as our experience. Each step took us further, building towards a dream that we would one day try to explain.

"But they came and prompted a tumultuous change. That is now the reality of our situation. We gobbled down grain and chaff. We took upon ourselves their ways, in a land that was no longer ours.

"Yes, father, we go in pursuit of those dreams, go after those elusive promises because now we are mere

14

expressions of that infinite desire for the chase. You abandoned us to their custody and now we have become crude imitations of them. They promised us places amongst them, if we renounced ourselves completely. Now we drift lost, somewhere between two people and two worlds."

The old man shook his head painfully. He would never be able to explain how his flashing fingers transformed *Nhemamusasa* into *Nyamamusango*. Farai followed with an unexpected wild passion. The hunters trudge on in the searing sun and come upon a herd of wildebeest at a watering hole. The young men, weighed down by two hard days of empty expectation, stampede blindly towards the herd. Alerted, the wildebeests gallop away throwing back their hind legs in mockery. The old men – especially VaGudza – look at the young men and shake their heads reproachfully. VaGudza sighs and motions the young men towards him. He lifts his left forefinger before beginning the drill: "You must develop the tactics of lions. They never allow the wind to carry their scent to their quarry. They don't just run: they study the situation first and when they have done so, the race is lightning and can be fatal. Lions also create decoys and play lethal games. But above all," VaGudza concluded, "lions hunt as a group, each animal playing its part in a series of linked actions that will result in a kill."

The edges of *Nyamamusango* began to crack. Farai's father stood up and feigned a hunter's dance, letting out a piercing "BAYA!" The song escalated. Farai's heart threatened to break away from his chest. The old man looked at him and past him at the hunters that had resumed their trek. They round a small kopje and . . . a herd of kudu! Tension. The hunters immediately become a pride of lions and crouch. Alerted, the herd stops grazing and stares at the lions in wide-eyed anxiety. The kudu bull emits a hoarse noise and stamps one of its forelegs on the ground. And then slowly, a whole series of connected action begins. When, at last, the final movement is complete, the youngest man in the expedition stands with one of his legs resting on the twitching head of the kudu bull with its massive twisted horns.

The music leapt and pulsated. The old man closed his eyes. There was only pain, a pain, interminable pain – pain even beyond the hunters.

And then somehow, he jabbed the lower key of his *mbira*, and plunged into another tune, *Mahororo,* the return. It was by far the most esteemed song, the unfolding of the expectations of those at home and the ending of the storm. The hunters are now outside the village carrying in the dried meat. The leader of the expedition, a young man, leads the way majestically. He walks in battle stance, holding his spear and shield. He was the one responsible for almost everything except scattering the sacred snuff to the winds before the start of the expedition. The older men did that. They also did something else. They were the ones who squatted under the *muhacha* tree and propitiated the ancestors with the blood of their first kill. But the young man would offer the prayers to the ancestral spirits just before the end of the expedition. This time, this young man was the leader; next time, another would take his place.

Inside the kraal a din erupts. Word has already reached the women that the men have returned. Drums start beating and there is ululation. The ground shakes as young women dance the welcome song.

"Father, there in no land. There are no people, there is no life. Our identity has been lost. The land is our identity. We have to reclaim it even if it means death. We have to join the liberation forces and fight to reclaim the land."

The old man gasped. The storm died, music and time too. He groped for his life and found it, slung it over his shoulders and walked wearily away to welcome his great-grandfather VaGudza and the returning hunters. Suddenly, an inexplicable feeling of urgency gripped him and he doubled his pace. He did not want to miss the celebrations, especially the welcome song and dance.

Scars

There is a path from our village that snakes through the valleys and gullies to the school on the other side of the rise. Each time I come home from the city, I walk along this path with the setting sun behind me. It is not the overwhelming mantle of gold from the lingering sun clothing the naked land that causes nostalgia. Neither is it the rhythmic preparation of the village for sleep: the cracking whips of the herdboys as they drive their cud-chewing herds home from the veld, the pealing laughter of the girls trading gossip at the village well, the disjointed song that Magaya, the village widower, sings as he trudges drunkenly home from one of Mai Dirayi's numerous beer parties to his painful loneliness. No, it is not any of this. It is something else, a painful memory. One day, I hope to meet a fifteen-year-old girl from all those years ago running home from primary school. That small girl holds the key to the emptiness in my life.

Perhaps she was beautiful but because we had virtually

grown up together, I did not know it. Perhaps the village knew. At school, we were not only in the same class, we sat at the same desk. Mrs Mano, our class teacher, teased us saying what a pair we made and we wondered. We were both too young to understand or care. We had a magic friendship, but because we were always together, we were not aware of it.

During morning breaks, we would sneak behind the anthill near the school garden and share roasted nuts or some other delicious seasonal morsel. One day, I stole half-a-crown from my mother's Methodist Church uniform and bought her some biscuits and sweets. Of course she did not know that I had stolen the money from my mother, but I wonder whether she would have cared even if she had known.

After school, we would come home through the harvested fields looking for groundnuts and cucumbers. And she would be carrying my books as I plucked the wild cucumbers from some cranny. Sometimes, it would be wild fruit, especially *mazhanje* and *nhunguru* from some small tree. Now, as I look back, perhaps she was beautiful but perhaps I was too young to know what this meant. Perhaps the village noticed or perhaps it was too busy with its daily chores to do so.

Then two traumatic things happened during the Christmas holidays after our Standard Six examinations. First, her parents separated. The village buzzed with gossip. Her mother was alleged to have done all sorts of things. Some said she was a witch who kept a hyena on the small hill overlooking the village and was responsible for every death that had occurred in the village. Others said she was sexually insatiable and slept with so many men that she alone knew who the real fathers of her three children were. The village took sides with Chipo's father. The children, especially Chipo, withdrew deeper and deeper into themselves as their father took a second wife. The Chipo that I knew changed into a shy, unsure and sullen girl, always silent and brooding.

The second thing was that we both went to secondary boarding schools and for the first time, we were without each other. To me, the abrupt separation and the disturbing experience of a new life in a strange place surrounded by unfamiliar faces, a place of rigid norms and values, compounded my sense of loneliness. Somehow I waited for the holidays and when they finally came, I suddenly did not know what I had been waiting for so anxiously. And so when I got to the village, I was confused. And I waited for Sunday and Chipo.

During service that Sunday, our eyes met but she quickly looked away. I did not know then that those eyes would stay with me, haunt me, plead with me, make me reverse nearly every decision that I have taken in my life. After the service we walked out of the school yard, past the school garden and down to the dry river-bed. She walked briskly ahead of me, never once looking back. She sat down on a fallen tree trunk. I came and sat beside her. And then she looked at me.

"Charles, if you love me, kiss me," she said. I was dumbfounded. "Charles, please kiss me," she said touching me. I did not understand the significance of what she was asking me to do. Then she began to cry. "How can the world be so unfair?" she continued. "I don't even know where my mother is and you, of all people, do not love me. No one in this world loves me." She stood up and started walking back to the village. I dazedly stood up and followed her. I did not understand anything.

Once back at school for the second term, I wrote her a letter reassuring her of my friendship. She did not reply. That term I wrote her four letters but she did not reply to any one of them. She told me during the next school holiday that she was sure I did not love her. She said it was all because she came from a broken home and because, as her step-mother had always told her, she would end up like her mother, a common slut and prostitute. She cried.

I also cried. And so, the delicate relationship continued.

We wrote to each other endlessly from our respective schools, I stating how foolish she was to think that I could not love her and she reiterating her position that I despised her after what happened on that fateful Sunday down by the dry river-bed. She also said that since my father owned a grinding mill, she did not see how the son of a businessman could love her. I did not understand how much reassurance she needed. How could I?

This awkward, painful dialogue continued into the following year until her father suddenly withdrew her from school. He said he did not have any more money to spend on her. She cried and wrote to me saying that since I was going to be very educated and she was not, there was no way we could care for each other. And just before I was about to give up, she wrote me a curious letter: "Forget about everything, Charles. When you come home, we will talk and settle everything."

It was only much later, after I had written my final A level examinations, that I began to understand. Everything changed then. Even the sun seemed reluctant to set. Our emotional journey had begun. I was a man. Chipo was a deep dark crater whose depths no one had ever reached. She would moan and gasp, urging me to descend deeper but I was afraid and that made her cry.

"What are you afraid of, Charles?" she asked me one day.
"I don't know," I answered.
"Then you don't love me."
"I do."
"Swear it."
"I love you, Chipo."

She drew her face closer to mine. My heart constricted. Her face was an infinitely rolling veld, her eyes the veld's sky and her tears the rain. . . I was caught in a storm on the veld of her face. I sought for shelter anywhere – under the trees, the hills, rocks, anthills, anywhere. Then I reached the crater. I plunged down its dizzying depth. I hurtled down, crying. Behind me, I could hear her gasping. Then the momentous crash and – discovery. Cool, soft sand here, cool, soft sand there and not a single human footprint to be seen. I stayed.

I sought shelter in her from numerous other storms. Then one day, she just disappeared from the village. I was baffled. I did not know what to do. Even her people did not know where she had gone. I was empty with disbelief. About a month later, her brother told me that she had gone to Harare and was staying with their mother. I wrote to her and she did not reply. I wrote to her again and this time, she replied in a short, indifferent letter. I wrote to her again and she replied saying that she wished I would not write such long, frequent letters. I was frantic. I had to see her.

All the way to the city, from Mutoko where I was doing temporary teaching six months later, Chipo's face was etched in my mind's eye: a veld clouded with numerous gathering storms. I didn't see the rolling tears. I felt them splash over me. I knew that the storms had broken. The gusts howled across my being, leaving me drenched. Chipo, my shelter, had gone.

I found the house in Highfield very easily. She was there. My heart lurched. She received me calmly and said she was surprised to see me. My God, how she had changed! She wore a pair of blue jeans and a matching sleeveless top. Her hair was plaited in dreadlocks falling down to her shoulders. Huge golden ear-rings dangled from either side of her head. For the first time, I felt unsure in my grey safari suit.

"This is my mother's house," she said without greeting me. And then, "By the way, how are you?"

She left me in the sitting room with a small boy and disappeared into one of the bedrooms. I waited. She returned some ten or so minutes later. "You should have told me that you were coming." I did not know whether this statement was a compliment or an accusation. I licked my dry lips. She sat down and folded her arms. Silence. She stood up and once again left the room. She came back immediately and sat down. The tension between us began to build up.

"I have been missing you, Chipo," I said.

"Really," she replied coldly, lacing and interlacing her fingers. "But let's get to the point, Charles. If you should visit me again in the future please let me know you are coming." Again, I did not know whether this was an accusation or a reminder but there was a chilly aloofness in her voice. I opened my mouth to say something but she cut me short.

"Some people are coming to pick me up," she looked at her expensive watch. Then she stood up and left the room. I swallowed.

Then I stood up, picked up my cheap briefcase and walked out. She did not come to the door to see me off.

It is a long time ago now, in fact years, and since then I have secured a clerical job in Harare. A lot of things have come and gone, but for me, all have been marred by futility – that miscarried marriage three years ago, for instance.

Back at the village, they say all sorts of things about Chipo. Some say she married a millionaire and her mother received and ate the lobola. Others say she has emigrated to Europe with her German boyfriend. There are also those who say her decomposed body was found in the Mukuvisi River murdered by one of the numerous men whose marriages she had helped to destroy. They say all sorts of things about her but for me, the only truth is the emptiness stretching before me.

There is a path from our village that snakes its way through the valleys and gullies to the school on the other side of the rise. Each time I come home from the city, I walk down that path. One day, I hope to meet a fifteen-year-old girl running home late from school. She holds the key to the emptiness in my life.

Who Killed the Twig-snake, Kangamiti?

I am still confused because even now Kudakwashe insists he did not see it first. Regardless of who did, the twig-snake caused quite a stir. Those of us who were engaged in a cut-throat game of tennis on the netball pitch rushed to the orchard where the snake was reported to be. When we arrived at the small lemon tree it was already surrounded by numerous others who had got wind of the news before us. For some obscure reason we all wanted to see the snake.

It lay straight and motionless across three branches of the small lemon tree. Its dark brownish colour merged flawlessly into that of the tree. Absolutely nothing suggested the snake could still be alive.

"It's dead!" Godfrey shouted above the excited murmur.

"It's alive!" cried more than a dozen voices.

"Kuda poked it and it writhed," said Jane, a Grade 6 classmate.

"Quite right, Jane!" shouted Kuda, enthralled. "If you seriously think it's dead, here you are. Try it," he said, holding out the stick.

"Come on, take it and try," someone shouted.

We all drew back.

Godfrey shot a scared glance at the stick and took two steps backwards. "I didn't say it wasn't alive," he whimpered.

"Okay, then let's kill it!" someone suggested.

Although Francis now denies he said it, everyone maintains he did. In my case I did not only hear him say it, I saw him say it. I couldn't be wrong; he was standing close to me.

And so, in response to Francis' exhortation, we all rushed to collect stones.

Although surprisingly Francis now says we threw the first stones, I deny that. What I remember is that when I threw my first stone, many others had already thrown stones.

In a very short time the job was done. But the snake's head, apparently unscathed, lay wedged between two stones. Its bluish, unblinking eyes shone as if in complete agreement with our task, as if we had relieved it of the burden of a lifetime. It opened its mouth, closed it, opened it again and closed it, like an exhausted octogenarian. Although Francis now vehemently denies it, it was after seeing this that I told him there was something unearthly about the snake.

If it had not been for the lemon tree perhaps the incident might have gone unnoticed. But Mr Moyo, our headmaster, had always stressed the need to preserve trees and plant new ones, and it was 'The Year of the Tree'. And by the time we had finished with Kangamiti, the twig-snake, the lemon tree had also been destroyed.

Although everyone – especially Francis – didn't like the idea, I immediately suggested we report the incident to the headmaster. I still maintain that this is what happened. Actually someone – I cannot remember who – said only a sell-out would do such a thing. So I didn't go to see the HM. But I did suggest the idea.

To most of us, how the headmaster came to know of the incident is still a mystery. The next day, hardly thirty minutes after morning break, our teacher announced that we were required at assembly. No one was particularly worried as this sometimes happened when a special announcement was to be made.

The headmaster wore the darkest face I had ever seen. He was angry. "Everybody sit down!" he barked at us.

We all sat down.

"Whilst the whole school has been busy planting and preserving trees in our school yard, certain vandals have set about stripping the orchard of its glory." His angry eyes scanned the rows in which we sat. It had been the first time I had heard the word 'vandal' and it added to my fright. "All those who participated in the killing of the snake in the orchard come to the front!" he ordered.

There was dead silence as we all looked around us. Then there was a rustle and Jane stood up. She walked right to the front: unashamedly. Chipo, Anna, Lizzie, Susan and Tendai followed and then the whole group. But I remained sitting on the floor of the hall, my eyes staring unseeingly at the ground. My heart lurched. My face felt hot. I felt I could hardly breathe.

"So you are the culprits." His voice was stern.

"Excuse me, sir," interjected Francis. "There are still some boys who haven't come to the front."

"There are still more of you?" queried the headmaster angrily.

With that awful sinking feeling I knew he meant me. I

stood up trembling and hobbled awkwardly to the front.

"You coward!" the headmaster exclaimed loudly. The whole school broke out laughing.

After everyone who'd thought they could get away with it had been discovered, the headmaster continued. "These are the people who mutilate our efforts. These are the people who destroy trees in the schoolyard. They are plunderers. They are not worthy of a place in this school." He paused.

"Only today they have destroyed a lemon tree in the orchard because they wanted to kill a snake." He paused. "Although I deplore what they have done, there is something else that concerns me. I am worried about the retaliation of the Winds."

We all looked at the headmaster, puzzled.

"The snake they have killed, Kangamiti, is a sacred snake. It is the royal courier of our ancestral spirits."

It took us a little while to grasp the implications of his words. As meaning sunk in, so too did panic.

The headmaster continued: "That snake should never have been killed. It never DIES. It isn't of *this* world." He stopped deliberately and looked at us. "The spirits of the deceased might decide to retaliate and punish those responsible." He seemed resigned to our fate.

Our spirits froze. We had never considered that the consequences of our offence could be so grave. We felt doomed. We had all heard of the retaliation of the Winds.

"Who saw the sacred snake first?" the headmaster asked.

No one dared to raise a hand.

"Lydia," the headmaster picked a name at random.

She stood up and began sucking her forefinger. Then she looked around and pointed a finger. "Kudakwashe."

Kudakwashe leapt up. "I didn't!" he said, fiercely remorseful.

"But you poked it with a twig," she insisted.

Kudakwashe licked his dry lips helplessly, looking about him like a trapped animal.

"He saw it first, sir," Godfrey said, standing up.

There was a general murmur of consent.

"I only poked it. I didn't see it."

"Quiet!" shouted Mr Moyo.

There was silence.

"Who said it should be killed?"

"Francis!" I said breathlessly, even before I could stand up.

Francis glared at me and then calmly stood up and said in a very controlled voice, "I don't remember ever saying anything like that."

His answer caught me unawares. I said shaking slightly, "I swear it was you, Francis!"

"It was Francis!" Jane entered the fray. I heaved a sigh of relief. But the interrogation wasn't over yet.

"And who killed the snake?" Mr Moyo asked.

No one answered. We had all thrown stones at it but who could say who the culprit was? Who could name the one person whose stone had actually killed Kangamiti?

Mr Moyo uttered a mirthless chuckle. "I know you all threw stones but the person who threw the stone that killed the snake is in trouble. When a snake such as this dies, a sacrifice of human blood will be immediately required." His voice was cheerless. He blew his nose. The worried look returned to his face. We all sat staring grimly ahead of us, grimly absorbing this new piece of information. "All right you may all go back to your classes," he said gloomily, and blew his nose again.

"I don't think it's fair for me or the school to make the situation out to be any worse than it already is for you. The Winds will settle that," he said ambiguously and then fell into an absolute silence.

Even as we shuffled back to our classes we felt we were as good as dead. Because I sat next to Francis in class his presence slightly relieved me; I was certain that his predicament was worse than mine.

Halfway through the lessons he staggered up to the teacher, sweating. It was obvious that he thought he was sick. Jane who sat in front of me heaved. Me too. The dice had been thrown.

But when later at lunch break we also learned that Kudakwashe had been taken by a sudden seeming illness we were puzzled. All the way home for lunch we walked in small groups, guardedly rehearsing the events of the day.

And when, the following morning, we saw Francis and Kuda pale but back at school, we felt a bit unsure. But when we saw them again the following morning, now positively fit, we no longer knew what to believe. Was it possible that Mr Moyo had not been telling the truth? Had he just intended to scare us when he said that the Winds would retaliate? Or could it be that They had forgiven us? We no longer knew what to believe.

Burdens

It was already long after midnight and everyone had left the shebeen except the morose long-distance truck driver who sat all by himself on a chair in the shadow cast by the peach tree against the township's tower light. He seemed to like to sit late and alone and now because it was very late and everyone had gone, it was quiet and that seemed to make him happy.

The two girls employed at the shebeen to sell beer and entertain clients watched him from the window of the kitchen where the deep-freeze stood and they saw that he was drunk but there was nothing they could do about it.

"They say he has got lots of money," said the taller one.

"Nonsense," said the shorter girl. "If he had, would he come here? I ask you?"

"He likes it here."

"Those with money don't drink here."

"But he likes it here."

"It's you that likes him. Do you think people can't see it?"

The taller one folded her arms across her bosom and looked out through the window at the empty chairs, except for the one where the solitary truck driver sat in the shadow of the peach tree. A dog started barking somewhere across the street and this prompted others throughout the township to bark in chorus. The noise was ugly, empty, continuous.

A heavy, long-distance truck thundered past the main road that ran along the edge of the township and the noise shook the night. The truck driver sitting alone in the shadow of the peach tree raised his eyes and looked towards the receding noise and he began playing with the glass of frothing beer with his fingers. He lifted his eyes again and looked in the direction of the main road and the dying sound of the truck. It seemed as if his thoughts had travelled to those distant places through which he sometimes passed.

"My boyfriend from Highfield is coming to see me next week," said the taller girl. "He has promised to marry me sometime next year."

"Who do you think you are fooling? Who else but you would believe such promises?" the other one said sarcastically.

"He has already introduced me to his sister in Mufakose."

"Even if he has, what would he do with a cheap prostitute who sometimes solicits men as old as her grandfather to take her home?"

"And he says we will have the biggest wedding the whole of Murewa has ever seen."

The shorter one pulled a disgusted face and looked away. The long-distance truck driver snapped his fingers for one more beer. The taller one moved over to him carrying a lager on a tray and put it down on the table in front of him. The driver paid, quietly filled his glass and stared thoughtfully at the frothing beer. The waitress went back into the kitchen.

"Does he want to drink all night?" the shorter one grumbled. "I want to sleep."

"He has got the money."

"Money is all you think about. I bet that sometimes you get laid for just a dollar," she said wanting to hurt the other girl as much as she could. "Every time he returns from one of his long trips to South Africa or Botswana, it means trouble for us."

"They say he survived a Renamo ambush on one of his trips to Malawi through Mozambique. They say he was the only survivor."

"I wish they had killed him. I want to sleep."

"I must get out of this place. I must," the taller one said emotionally.

"And where would you go? Back to Murewa to the bickering of your father's sister's son who took over your mother after your father died? Is that what you want to do?" the shorter one snapped. "Anyway, what's stopping you? Why don't you pack your old suitcase and leave? No one will miss you."

The truck driver took one long swig of his beer and asked for another. The taller girl picked up her tray and took him the beer. He quietly filled his glass and stared morosely at the frothing liquid. The waitress returned to the kitchen.

The driver continued staring unseeing at his beer and looked towards the main road where the sound of the long distance truck had long since died away.

"He never seems to get drunk."

"He drinks every day."

"How do they say he survived the ambush?"

"Why don't you ask him? You were out there with him just a moment ago."

"When he eventually got home after that trip, he must

have brewed beer for his ancestors."

"Why don't you just say you wish you had been the one to brew that beer. Why don't you ask him to take you home tonight to infect him with the Aids that you've contracted from your numerous soldiers?"

The driver began to doze and both girls noticed it.

"I am going over to tell him to go home," said the shorter one.

"The madam will not be happy with that. He might wake up and buy more beer."

"Blast you and your madam. I want to sleep."

"I want to get away from this place."

"No one will miss you," the shorter one laughed derisively.

"They say his wife ran away from him."

"What person but you would want to stay with a man like that?"

"They say she ran away because he was unable to make her pregnant."

"I bet he just went home stone drunk each day and slept like a log. Women are not married to eat sadza." She swallowed. "Perhaps you would stay, just for the money."

"How did he survive the ambush?"

"Why don't you ask him?"

"But the funniest thing is that he has children by another marriage."

"She was clever. I would do that to him; give him the fruit of other men's loins." She shot an angry look at the dozing driver. "O God, how I want to sleep. Why wasn't he killed in the ambush?"

"If he has children from another marriage then he couldn't have failed to make her pregnant."

"Why should that bother you?" the smaller one shouted, tired beyond belief.

The truck driver woke up with a start, looked at his glass and then asked for one more beer. The taller one hurried over to him with a lager on her tray. She wiped the table with a towel and smiled at the driver. He accepted the beer sullenly and looked away. The waitress hurried back into the kitchen.

"What did you say to him?"

"They say he occupies a single room in another shebeen at the extreme end of the township."

"You smiled at him. I saw you."

"When I finally get married, I will have only three children."

"Why did you smile at him?"

"Children are so expensive; three is actually a burden."

"Did he promise to take you home tonight?"

"And I would send them to the nicest school in the country."

"If they are not bright, it won't be my fault."

"Are you not ashamed of yourself for soliciting men?"

"I won't be doing it so that they will look after me. No."

"You are a disgrace!"

"But if they should decide to care for me, that would be fine."

"You are a disgraceful slut!"

"I want to get away from this place."

"I want to go to bed."

The truck driver snapped his fingers for one more beer and the shorter one said she would take it to him this time. The taller one sat down heavily on the chair inside the kitchen and tried to drive away the sleepiness that was engulfing her.

She listened to the massaging drawl of the deep-freeze motor and thought how soothing it was. She edged closer to the noise as if for comfort and suddenly, she became a song drifting and blowing in the wind. The song became a wedding song, her wedding song. What the village could not understand was why there was no groom. She was marrying herself! Just before her mother began to weep, she woke up and looked about her. The truck driver had gone. So too had her workmate. She went into the small room that they both shared. She was not there. She flung herself on to the mat on the floor and began to cry wishing that somebody would help her to get away from the rotten place. In the main bedroom, the madam, taking an unusual break from her nocturnal escapades, mumbled something in her sleep.

Septic Wounds

The little boy, Taurayi, sped across the yard and retrieved the letter from the letter-box. He scrutinized it, especially the capital letter 'M,' and he immediately knew where it came from: Uncle Petros or Comrade Zvenyika as he was popularly known. The little boy ran back to the house and gave the letter to his mother. Mrs Maruta slit open the envelope, took out the letter, read it and sighed.

"Does he say he's coming?" Taurayi asked breathlessly.
"Who?" asked his mother rather surprised.
"Comrade Zvenyika."

"How did you guess?" The little boy grinned and looked away. "Well, he says tomorrow," she answered rather dejectedly. Taurayi jumped triumphantly into the air and sped out of the room as if to meet his uncle. Left behind, Mrs Maruta re-read the letter and sighed. She took it to her husband in the bedroom.

He read the letter and grunted. He read the letter again and made further guttural sounds. Then he threw his legs off the creaking bed and stood up. His wife looked away.

"There is no need to look like that just because you already know how I feel about him."

"But he is your only brother, Cephas!" There was pain in her voice.

"Yes, he is my brother, but you know where and how our paths cross. He's just a big mouth with his endless yapping about battles in Buhera – or was it Bikita? – during that lousy war. Who still wants to hear about all that? Why doesn't he put that period behind him? Show me a thousand crazy people and I will show you just one!"

"He's *not* crazy. That's far too simple."

"Simple! Did you say 'simple'?" he snorted. "This time, I'm going to tell him right to his face what a yawn he is. Enough is enough. We can't go on pretending that we enjoy his stupid stories. And what's more, can you tell me how long my mother and father will have to cook for him? A man going on forty and still unmarried! Will you also try and tell me that the war was responsible for this?" He stormed out and banged the door behind him.

The little boy heard it all from behind the house and wondered. His thoughts drifted away and dissolved in the afternoon haze. The township, Warren Park, lay silent and subdued, as if it were waiting for the unwelcome arrival of Comrade Zvenyika.

Scattered white clouds raced confusedly across the sky tripping and tumbling in each other's path. Taurayi's thoughts freed themselves from the clouds and drifted on, past the weakly flickering red light that came from Heroes Acre, as he tried to understand something which got lost in the meanderings of his mind. Then he shrugged his little shoulders and walked away.

Comrade Zvenyika arrived the following afternoon. The

first person to see him was the little boy who saw his uncle hobbling down the street and recognized him immediately from his crutches, his amputated leg, his broad-brimmed hat festooned with a leopard skin and the canvas travelling bag slung on his shoulder like a gun. Of all his scanty possessions he treasured his hat the most, and wore it only on special occasions such as going to collect his monthly War Victims' compensation, weddings, going to the cattle-dip and coming to Harare. The hat was his prize possession.

The little boy ran up the street and into the warmth of his uncle's outstretched arms and hearty laughter and then he asked the little boy to carry his canvas bag. Taurayi was the only person he allowed to carry his bag and even sometimes to wear the hat. This time he allowed him not only to carry the bag but also to wear his hat and so they walked side by side back to the house.

"Growing bigger and bigger aren't you? Very soon, the hat won't fit you anymore." The little boy blushed. "How is everyone at home?"

"We're fine. I'm going to primary school now."

His uncle laughed lightly. "School," he said. "That reminds me of something. We were once attacked at a school in Buhera. I survived by pretending to be one of the teachers."

"Did you?" the child's eyes widened.

"Yes, one had to be resourceful to survive. And it was worse if one was the commander, and I was."

"You will tell me the story of how you lost your leg, Uncle, won't you?"

"Well, we'll see. Those are stories for men." He paused. "But then why not? Perhaps this time I will tell you." They walked on towards the house. The location stood still with its hands on its hips and its eyes following them silently. Mrs Maruta came to the gate to meet them.

Later that afternoon when Comrade Zvenyika's younger brother, Cephas, arrived home from work, he walked past his elder brother without even looking at him and immediately shut himself in the bedroom. Comrade Zvenyika wondered if his brother had actually seen him. It was hard to believe he hadn't. The injured man swallowed and rubbed the stumpy end of his amputated leg with his hand.

After what seemed a very long time, his younger brother emerged from his room whistling, and without looking at his elder brother, exclaimed: "O-oh so it's you? I didn't see you when I came in. Mai Taurayi told me that she had had your letter the other day. When did you arrive?"

The older man felt, as he always did, an erosion of certainty and he steeled himself against it, against the sense of inadequacy which threatened to engulf him. His younger brother kept his face averted as if the older man was of no importance, no value at all.

Comrade Zvenyika swallowed, wishing he was somewhere else. When he felt like this, he knew he must withdraw into the background and only answer questions that were put to him. When all the routine replies had been given then came a very strange question: "How is Amai Chipo?" asked the younger man in a cold detached voice. Comrade Zvenyika was puzzled. Amai Chipo was a notorious prostitute at their village in Mhondoro.

"I haven't seen her for a long time," he answered.

"Have they started the food-for-work programme yet?" Cephas cruelly asked, feeling a vindictive satisfaction as he crudely stated his question.

"Not that I know of," his elder brother replied. Then silence fell.

Much later, still softly whistling under his breath and never having looked at his brother, Cephas left.

Comrade Zvenyika continued rubbing the stumpy end

of his amputated leg with his hand.

During supper that evening, Mai Taurayi tried to cheer everyone up paying particular attention to Comrade Zvenyika. The man, who was visibly upset, slowly began to feel better and began to enjoy his steak. Cephas ate silently, hunched over his plate, as if the meal were an ordeal. The little boy felt the tension and stole furtive glances at his uncle, his father and his mother.

"Travelling all the way here has whetted my appetite," said the older man between mouthfuls. "It reminds me of when we were crossing the Devure Ranch along the Save River. Eight days of hard unbroken walking left us with blisters on our feet and in-between our thighs and a huge appetite. Once we got to Bikita on the other side of the ranch, each of us felt he could devour a goat," he laughed. His younger brother kept eating without raising his head.

"That's the trouble with hunger," said Mai Taurayi. "It has its own measure." The younger brother glanced at his wife. She looked away. Comrade Zvenyika, who had not noticed the exchange, laughed again a little recklessly.

Then he stopped eating and his eyes acquired an animated glimmer. His lips began to tremble. The little boy saw it and knew the sign. He saw his uncle's nostrils flare a little and he knew that sign too. "I remember once, on our way from Mozambique, we had a platoon of freshly trained recruits and I was the commander. I warned them against eating all their rations too quickly but they did not pay any heed to me. They drank all their water and ate all their tinned food," he chuckled again. "You should have seen them! On Devure Ranch they drank their urine!"

He paused and pushed away his plate as if it would get in the way of his story. "Mind you there was always a danger of the Rhodesians picking up our spoor and tracking us down. We had to get away from that damn area as quickly as we could and eight days was the fastest we could make it."

As his father gulped down his glass of water, the little boy saw the anger in his eyes. He watched his father put his empty glass down carefully, too carefully. He watched his mother put more meat on his uncle's plate and push it back in front him.

The little boy watched his uncle and saw his lip twitch. He also saw his eyes shine like stars and his nose flare.

"I was just wondering," Comrade Zvenyika said. "I was just wondering if I ever told you how one day, Lazarus, our most reliable *mujibha* walked us straight into a Selous Scout ambush?"

His younger brother banged the table with a clenched fist. "You have told us that lousy story more than five times already!"

"Really? You could be right," Comrade Zvenyika said quietly. The little boy watched him rub the stumpy end of his amputated leg with the palm of his hand.

"I want to hear the story again," the little boy heard himself exclaiming. His father banged the table with his fist, fixed the little boy with a look and pointed towards the open door to the kitchen. Taurayi stood up sheepishly and disappeared. Then the younger man turned around and looked at his elder brother for the first time.

"Why do you always force everyone to endure your boring stories about a war that ended almost a generation ago? You fought in it all right, but now it's over. Why do you have to keep telling us over and over again all about it, as if it happened yesterday? We are all thoroughly tired of it and besides we have our own rather different views about that stupid war." His wife opened her mouth to speak but said nothing. "Look at you," he continued. "You lost your leg and what did you get for it? Not even a thank you. Just a paltry monthly allowance and they almost refused you that until we spent a lot of money proving that the injury happened during the war." The older man looked away to hide his pain. The woman opened her mouth to speak and said nothing.

"Mukoma, these are facts that I am telling you. You deserved more. We all deserved more than these everlasting queues and endless shortages of almost every basic commodity" He paused. "And whilst you fought, some people unashamedly made money out of that war. And now, whilst you continue to talk, other people are making their millions. Is it your job just to talk and talk?"

"Please don't be so cruel, Cephas," his wife said at last.

"I am not being cruel. I am telling him the truth."

Comrade Zvenyika stood up, collected his crutches, hobbled out and sat in the dull light on the veranda, staring unseeingly out into the darkness. The man and the woman watched him silently. Taurayi saw him through the open window of the kitchen and went to join him.

"Will you tell me the story now that we are all alone?" he implored. His uncle shook his head dejectedly.

"It's not that important after all. We have to forget about the war."

"Please, Uncle!"

The older man rubbed the stumpy end of his leg with the palm of his hand, his face and eyes lost all expression. He could have been talking to himself. "It's not because I was the section commander, no. There were a thousand or more others throughout the operational zones. Perhaps it is because of the uniqueness of that experience. No one forced anybody to go to war yet we all went knowing quite well that we might die. Most of us went there knowing that we would not receive any pay. That's what's important. To many of us, that war was the single most important thing to happen in our otherwise empty lives. It was that and much more besides.

"To the majority of us, the war seemed infinite, without end. We never imagined it would end within our own lifetimes. The war embedded itself in us. It became the most real part of our lives. And so we saw the Lancaster House Conference as just another talking shop – there had been so many before. Then, suddenly, the war had ended. No one could believe it. And now still, a decade later, in the communal areas there are scores of bewildered men just like me who still haven't got over the shock not of the war, but of the end of the war. Yes, Taurayi, your father is right. We must get over that damn war," he said heavily.

"But just one more time," the little boy implored.

"Yes, just one more time, Comrade Zvenyika," said his younger brother's wife, emerging from the house.

"Yes, Uncle, you were the commander and you did not want your men to get killed. How did you get out of that Selous Scout ambush? Just one more time. One day I also want to be a hero."

"Not hero," corrected his mother, "soldier."

Comrade Zvenyika rubbed his palms together and stared into the gloom. He started fiddling with his fingers like a small boy. "Yes," he stammered, "I had to save the boys but unfortunately, out of the twelve, seven died in that ambush and as for the commander . . . " he looked down at his amputated leg and sighed. Mai Taurayi began to cry. The little boy looked at both of them and struggled with the tears welling in his eyes. He looked past them, at the lonely flickering red light of Heroes Acres and failed to understand something. The township lay silent and subdued as if it was waiting for the arrival of another unwelcome visitor.

The Black Christ of Musami

I met him by accident on the small path between Musami Mission and the village to the east, somewhere near the Shavanhohwe River where my uncle lived and I knew immediately that I had met him somewhere before. There was something painfully familiar about his exhausted smile, the sad eyes and their distant, bruised look, as if they saw beyond this world.

"Have you forgotten me?" he asked in that detached voice and I remembered him. Yes, it was the voice that I had been hearing every day, every day since that bizarre encounter nearly two decades ago, during a pitched battle at the height of the liberation war, a battle in which we had been completely routed and our position overrun.

The attack had taken us by complete surprise at our makeshift base on the foot of the small hill near Saint Mary's Mission in Mount Darwin. The fierce air bombardment of our positions was immediately followed by a heavy ground assault and the fighting quickly spread and crossed the dry Bopoma River. Then it spilled into a village to the east of the Mission where several huts exploded in palls of black smoke, got stuck there briefly as the helicopters pounded their gunships into the village, crossed the main road to Mount Darwin and finally got lost in the thick bush near the Mazowe River, that river. We were completely encircled.

I clutched my rifle and kept running in long loping strides alongside Comrade Tichatonga. If only we could get to the river.

Above us, the thundering noise of the helicopters flying in ominous circles made the earth under our feet shake and tremble, and left the whole countryside vibrating. We kept under cover of the thick bush and ran on. If only we could get to the river. Then Tichatonga screamed, stumbled and fell, clutching his stomach. The bullet had cut across him leaving half his bowels hanging out. I knelt down and stuffed the damn things back in, tore his shirt and tied it around his abdomen to try and hold in what was coming out whilst he writhed and groaned in agony. There was nothing to understand. Then I heaved him over my shoulder and trudged onwards towards the river, that river.

It was then that I came face to face with him, his machine gun pointed menacingly at me and the sun playing on his greenish-brown Rhodesian Army camouflage. I froze with fear and my AK rifle slipped to the ground.

"Pick it up," he said calmly, as if he was a disinterested observer. I bent to pick up my gun staring all the while into the cold muzzle of his gun. Tichatonga groaned in pain.

"Now pass on," he said but I kept standing as if rooted to the ground. "I said pass on," he exclaimed angrily, as if his patience was exhausted. "There is no time to waste."

In a bewildered daze I shuffled on.

"Not that way," he called after me. "There are some of us there. Go to your right.

"I did as he had instructed. There was absolutely nothing to understand. Unsurely I kept looking back and angrily he kept waving me on. And behind me, the deafening sound of the helicopters receded further and further away.

By the time I reached the river, Tichatonga had died and I was dripping with sweat and soaked in blood, his blood. I cried. But I was not weeping for Tichatonga. I was weeping for the fate of my other six comrades whose whereabouts I did not know. (I later learned that five had been killed and the sixth wounded and captured.) I crossed the river and buried the body of Tichatonga in a cave in a hill near the river. This horrible, horrible war! Damn it! But the haunting words of the Rhodesian rifleman telling me to pass on, echoed and re-echoed in my mind, following me, haunting me, confusing me right through the war until the day that I met him, that same man with the detached voice, that man with the sad eyes and bruised look, on a shady path between Musami Mission and the village where my uncle lived, somewhere in Murewa, a long distance away from Saint Mary's Mission and over a decade later: that man.

"Have you forgotten me?" he asked again.

"I remember," I answered back. He smiled. I was overwhelmed for a moment. I did not know what to say or do. Should I thank him, and if I did, how would I do it? Would that immense act of kindness that had happened more than a decade ago be sufficiently acknowledged by the mere words, 'Thank you'? I was confused. What did he expect me to say or do for him? He hugged me like some long-lost-just-found friend and my anxious hidden turmoil intensified.

"You don't stay around here. Where are you going?" he asked me.

"Yes, no, I don't." I have come to see my uncle," and I gave him my uncle's name and said where he lived.

"You don't visit each other very frequently, do you?"

"Why?"

"He moved to another village not far from here several years ago. I will take you there." There he was again, that man, offering to help me. Would there ever be an end to his helping hand? And would I ever be able to reciprocate?

"You don't have to go out of your way to do that," I said nervously. "Just give me the directions and I am sure I will find my way."

He smiled. My god, that exhausted smile again, those sad eyes and their bruised distant look. Then it all seemed like yesterday, the memory of Tichatonga's sickening warm bowels, me trying to stuff them back inside: that horrible war and the mysterious Rhodesian rifleman. I didn't even know his name!

"My name is Godfrey Munetsi," he said as if he was reading my mind. I looked at him suspiciously.

"That was quite some time ago," I heard myself saying, referring to the war.

"Just like yesterday," he said. I grew tense. Somehow, I could feel that slowly we were coming face to face with that incident in that horrible war. Why had he let me through that fatal circle of Rhodesian soldiers?

And again, as if he was reading my mind, he deliberately changed the subject.

"Your uncle is not home by the way."

"He will come. He promised to meet me there. It's important."

"He is not coming."

"How do you know that?" I looked at him suspiciously again.

46

"I know," he said calmly, leading me towards the village where he said my uncle now lived. Damn uncle, I said to myself. And damn this man, I cursed silently. It was important that my uncle came. He was the reason why I had come all this way, using the little money that I had been given when they had retrenched me at the shoe factory. That was the place where my sister had helped me secure a job as a Kardex clerk after returning from the war that we had won about a decade ago. Why had my uncle promised to meet me if he knew he might not be able to travel from Mutare, where he worked as a factory supervisor in some paper-milling company? Why indeed? But how did this fellow know that he was not coming anyway?

"He is certainly not coming," he said suddenly. "And he might not be able to help you after all."

I looked at him, feeling my confusion growing.

"And don't blame him," he continued calmly. "Things are difficult these days and, you know, he doesn't own that factory."

"What are you talking about?" I asked him, visibly alarmed by his allusions.

"It all depends on what you want to see him about. If it's employment, I can help you."

There he was again, that man, with his outstretched hand, as if he was my personal Messiah, the man from that horrible war. It was employment that I wanted to see my uncle about. Our eyes met and I looked away from him, afraid. The man, where did he come from?

"I come from around this place, in Chibwe village next to the Mission."

I looked at him again. What sort of a person was he?

"When you go back to Harare, go to Zimbabwe Electric Industries along Lytton Road and ask to see Mr Vincent Ncube. Tell him I sent you. He will help you." He took my hand and looked at me. It seemed like yesterday all over again. The war, the agonized groaning of Tichatonga and the man telling me to move on when he could have mowed me down with his machine gun. "That is the home of your uncle across the stream. I had better return but please, don't forget to do as I tell you when you get back to Harare." It was as if he was pleading with me. I sighed.

"Why are you doing all this for me?" I asked, and then I broke down with the weight of memories. When at last I took hold of myself, the man had gone; the man from that awful battle.

All the way from Chitungwiza to the city to see Mr Vincent Ncube two days later, all the way in the fetid, overcrowded bus, through the massive grey sprawl that was the dormitory town with its unbreakable hold on poverty, past Nyatsime College, a futile symbol of hope and escape, across the Mhanyame River, I played hide and seek with the memory of the man from the horrible war, all the way to the city. I had reversed my initial resolve not to go and see Mr Ncube and I did not know why. Perhaps it was out of some desperate desire to reciprocate, to pay something back; perhaps it came from a strange sense of surrender; perhaps from curiosity; perhaps it was none of this but something else. I suddenly did not know and I felt I did not know anything.

I found the place very easily. Mr Ncube, the Personnel Manager, was there.

"You say you were referred to me by a Godfrey Munetsi from Musami. I don't know anyone by that name. I have never been to Murewa in my life, let alone Musami."

"But he talked about you."

"That's strange," Mr Ncube said, "but anyway," he continued, "one of our guys here, a Kardex clerk, resigned without notice two days ago and we shall advertise for another one through the papers some time this week. Have you got any qualifications in that line?"

My god, that man!

That Mr Ncube said he did not know anyone by the name of Godfrey Munetsi worried me. Each day as I worked through my schedule in the dispatch department, the memory of that man haunted me. Was he real or was he a creation of my own mind? The more I thought of him, the more confused I became.

Then one day, several months later in the workers' canteen, I overheard two men talk about Musami.

"Do either of you guys come from Musami?" I asked anxiously.

"I do. Why?" asked the shorter one.

"My uncle stays there."

"Where exactly?"

"I am not familiar with the names. I have only been there once. It's pretty close to the Mission."

"I come from Chibwe village."

My heart lurched. Wasn't that where the man from the war said he had come from? I became excited and the short fellow from Chibwe village noticed it.

"Why all the excitement?"

"There is someone I know who comes from that village."

"Not your uncle?"

"No. Someone else. Godfrey Munetsi."

"Someone you knew and not someone you know," he said dismissively. "It's almost ten years since he died," he concluded.

"What?" I exclaimed, standing up.

"Why?" he asked, astounded by my reaction.

"Did you say he had died?" I asked breathlessly.

"Yes, he died. He was my cousin. Most of us advised him to quit the regime's army but he wouldn't listen. Poor fellow. The war was almost over, when he came home for the weekend, just a few months before the cease-fire. He had never done so before. Little wonder that our ancestors and elders say that death lures us on. It was stupid of him in any case. The guerrillas got wind of his presence from

49

the local *mujibhas* and they shot him. He was left in the sun in the middle of the village for nearly a week. The whole village stank of his decomposing corpse.

"When the guerrillas finally gave us permission, we heaped together what still remained of him and buried that, our faces screwed up in disgust. . . against the body not the man. It took me years to eat meat again," He winced as if he would vomit. "He should never have come home."

"Are you quite certain he died," I whispered, sweat forming all over my body.

"*Shamwari,* he was MY cousin. Is there something wrong with you?"

"No," I said quickly. "Nothing," I continued as if to reassure myself. But nothing was the same any longer. I asked for two days' leave, went home, closed myself in the single room that I rented and sobbed. I was not weeping for anybody. I was weeping for myself. This sudden intense emotion, the weeping, released most of the awful tension that had built up inside me and I returned to work greatly relieved.

There was a huge old *mukamba* tree watching silently over our home from a small hill in the east which never seemed to shed any of its brittle, evergreen leaves. It was a towering giant that marked our home from miles around. Each time I came home from the city, I went up the hill and crouched under the tree, talking to it, talking to my deceased grandfather, asking him to allow the man from Musami to come and rest in the old man's silent, protective gaze. Each time I asked, the wind would blow, slowly stirring the massive tangled branches, as if gently agreeing to my strange request.

The Men in the Middle

When the Selous Scouts arrived at the rural business centre that day, their polished AK rifles glittering in the gold of the setting sun, people knew immediately that they were not freedom fighters, but there was nothing that they could do about it. They not only knew that they were imposters by their polished rifles, they also knew this from their clean blue jeans, their shifty eyes and their silence. They were not genuine and the people watched them helplessly.

They entered VaHungwe's bottle store at the end of the line of shops and lounged on the empty crates of beer, their weapons leaning against the nearby wall. VaHungwe's daughter, Coleta, emerged from behind the wooden counter and fearfully approached them to take their free order. Her father watched apprehensively, holding his breath. They all asked for Lions.

"There is only Castles," the girl said timidly.
"What the hell does that mean?" snapped their leader.

"The truck broke down last week," VaHungwe intervened from behind the counter, panic in his voice.

"How the hell does the truck get into this?" the leader
snapped again. The old man opened his mouth to say
something, gave up and shrugged his shoulders.

"There is also Milk Stout," the girl said.

"To hell with whatever you have. We want Lions!"
barked the leader. VaHungwe watched helplessly. This
was already a disastrous encounter. Inside it was getting
dark and he lit a spirit lamp.

"Have you got Stuyvesant?" the leader asked.

"There is only Players Gold Leaf," the girl said.

"To hell with Players. I want Peter Stuyvesant."

"The truck broke down last week," the old man pleaded.

"I don't see how the truck gets into this," retorted the
leader angrily.

At last the so-called guerrillas settled grudgingly for
Castles and Gold Leaf. They drank and smoked in silence.
VaHungwe and his daughter watched them anxiously,
trapped behind the wooden counter. Everyone at the
business centre knew that the Selous Scouts had closed in
on VaHungwe's bottle store and they watched the place
suspiciously through the darkness, wondering what could
be going on.

When they were drunk, the leader staggered forward
and rested his elbows on the counter. "Do you know who
we are?" he asked.

"No," the old man answered.

"Haven't you ever heard of freedom fighters?"

"I have."

"What do you think about them?"

The old man sighed heavily. He did not know what to
say.

"Yes, what do you think about us?"

"Well. . . I don't know," he stammered.

"You don't know? What do you mean you don't know?"

The leader was getting visibly angry. "Hell! Don't you know that there is a war going on?"

"Yes I know but the truth is I don't know."

"You are lucky it's someone else who is going to die tonight."

"Who is going to die?" the old man asked shakily.

"Mudhara Jera."

"VaJera?"

"His son is with the army. In fact, with the notorious Selous Scouts."

"But you. . . "

"But what?"

"I don't know."

The leader asked for another free crate of Castle and staggered back, and once again they resumed drinking and smoking in silence. They only stood up to relieve themselves on the walls behind the bottle store. VaHungwe watched them, worried by many things. He was worried about himself: what would the other people think about him . . . entertaining Selous Scouts? He knew they were not real guerrillas. If, on the other hand, VaJera got killed, would he not be thought to have played a hand in it? If only he could warn him perhaps he could save him. He turned his back to the Selous Scouts and conveyed this message with his eyes to his daughter. The girl nodded her assent.

The old man asked the leader of the so-called guerrillas if his daughter could go and roast them some meat. The leader said yes and the girl left.

Outside, the light from the spirit lamp shone eerily through the open door and onto the muddy puddles formed by the rain beyond the veranda. The night was deathly quiet. Once out of the light, the girl walked briskly up the line of shops towards VaJera's house at the end of the row. People heard her footsteps from behind their barricaded doors and peeped out at her on the dark street and knew that something was wrong. She walked up to VaJera's house and knocked on the door.

"Who is it?" a voice asked from inside.

"It's me, Coleta, VaHungwe's daughter." There was a moment's hesitation before the door creaked open.

"Is everything all right?" asked VaJera's wife letting Coleta in.

"Is *baba* in?" the girl asked.

"Yes," she said indicating a closed door. "What is the matter? Baba vaTinashe! There is someone to see you."

"Let her in here," VaJera said from behind the closed door. He lay on the bed with his clothes on and his head resting on a pile of pillows. "What is it?" he asked reluctantly. He knew that whatever she said would make no sense. The whole war now confused him. One never knew who was on whose side and for how long.

"A group of Selous Scouts is over at our place," the girl explained in a whisper. The man listened without saying anything. "They say they have come to kill you." The man continued looking at the opposite wall across the room and said nothing. "There are eight of them and they are heavily armed. They said they want to kill you because your son Tinashe is with the army's notorious Selous Scouts."

"Well, there is nothing I can do about it," he replied blankly, looking despairingly across the room. His wife stood numbly by as if the gravity of the situation had not yet reached her.

"Father thought I had better alert you."

"Go and thank him for me," he said adjusting his mound of pillows.

"Aren't you going to do anything?" the girl asked, dismayed.

"What can I do?"

"Run away somewhere."

"Run away where?"

"Anywhere safe. The city for instance."

"They will follow me there."

"Then run away into the forest to the comrades."

"Tinashe is with the army."

The girl shrugged her shoulders helplessly. "Well, I had better go back. I am supposed to be roasting meat." As she went out she saw VaJera lying on his bed staring blankly across the room at the opposite wall.

The Selous Scouts did not wait for their meat for, suddenly, an inexplicable urgency gripped them. They held their weapons at the ready and disappeared in the dark towards VaJera's house at the end of the row of shops.

They walked in single file between the rows of shops, their leader at the front. Most of them walked with a drunken wobble and the leader muttered to himself, his head down. It seemed as if he were conducting an argument, and occasionally he clenched his fists and threw his hands into the air as if he were being threatened by another point of view.

Behind their firmly closed doors, the people listened helplessly to the sounds outside, knowing that such movements in the dark were usually followed by a death.

"Did you see him?" VaHungwe asked his daughter anxiously.

"Yes, but I doubt whether he ever left his place."

"Why?"

"He didn't seem to have the will to do anything."

"What's got over him? They will kill him, the bastard."

"I don't know."

"The fool, they will surely kill him. And what will everyone think of us? Let's get away from this place," he said scrambling out towards their living quarters behind the bottle store.

By the time that the single shot that killed VaJera shattered the dark silence, VaHungwe, his wife and their two daughters were already behind the hill to the west of

55

the school and only a stone's throw away from the river. They were clutching all that they could of their belongings.

"Where are we going?" the wife asked the husband from behind.

"I don't know," the man replied, doubling his pace. So-called guerrillas killing the father of a Selous Scout, how would it all end.

Things We'd Rather Not Talk About

Perhaps if Paul Gavi had not suddenly realized that he had forgotten to bring the bottle of medicine he had got from that traditional healer years ago, it might have taken longer to come. Perhaps it might never have come at all. Now, as he sat in the back of the emergency taxi going from Mbare Bus Terminus into the city, he felt it coming in slow suffocating spasms. He swallowed, fighting it. If only he could get to the city, his mother's brother, who worked in a bank and was aware of the problem, would help him. He kept fighting it as it slowly closed in on him.

By the time he was dropped off along Robert Mugabe Road, he was soaked in sweat and for a moment, he thought he would make it to the bank. He half ran as the pounding footsteps behind bore down on him for the final onslaught. He fled blindly, letting out a piercing scream and dashed into a nearby hardware store for refuge. The startled Indian shop owner stared at him in wide-eyed disbelief.

"They are following me!" Paul screamed, ducking behind him. "Please don't let them take me."

"Who?" asked the shop owner.

"Can't you see them there at the door?"

"There is no one there," said the bewildered shopkeeper.

"They have all got in now," Paul said grabbing an axe from a shelf in self-defence but it was already too late.

Amos, the youth leader, approached him slowly, a menacing leer hanging on his thick, cracked lips. His bloodshot eyes never blinked: not once.

"You thought you could hide there in Salisbury whilst we fought the war for you here in the bush, a war that your father is unashamedly selling-out? But the comrades have got him at their base and now they want you."

Paul could not understand anything. Only the whirring receding sound of the bus that had just dropped him at the village bus stop seemed to make sense.

"We are wasting time comrades," said another youth emerging from the bushes. "Let's go. Everyone is waiting."

"But I also send watches and jeans from the city," Paul said.

"But I also send watches and jeans," the youth leader mimicked. "The trouble with you people whose parents own small stores is that you think you can fool anybody."

"I can't understand you. My brother is out there with the comrades in Mozambique. How can my family's commitment to the war be questioned?"

The youth leader slapped him viciously across the face. "Your father's store is used by the soldiers to send out telephone messages to various camps across the district. We razed it to the ground last night and the comrades have got the sell-out there with them. Let's go." There was nothing to understand.

The whole village was at the guerrilla base down the dry river-bed, and the atmosphere was charged. The guerrilla section commander, who seemed abnormally agitated issued orders and counter-orders brandishing his automatic weapon. The villagers sang an ominous song that told of the grim fate that befell sell-outs and enemy collaborators. Paul's father sat in front of them with his hands tied behind his back and his legs bound together with a piece of leather strapping. His eyes were puffed up and swollen. His lips were cut and he kept spitting out globules of dark-brown blood. It seemed he was breathing with great difficulty.

The guerrilla deputy commander, who appeared less agitated, whispered something in Paul's father's ear. The section commander who did not seem to like it beckoned his deputy and talked to him, making firm gestures with his clenched fists. The deputy shrugged his shoulders, shook his head and moved away. The villagers kept on singing.

"Bring the sell-out into the middle," the commander ordered. Two youths dragged Paul's father forward. The commander moved over to him and rammed his boot into the sides of the sell-out. The sell-out groaned and writhed. The deputy commander looked away, shaking his head helplessly. Paul's eyes met those of his mother in the crowd and they both looked away.

The commander asked: "Has the son from the city arrived?" The youth leader answered yes.

"Good. Bring him here."

Paul was dragged before the guerrilla commander. The commander looked at him and asked: "You got our letter?" and Paul answered yes. The commander continued looking at him and his lips slit into a grin. "Bring the axe and give it to him," he said. The deputy commander shrugged his shoulders and shook his head helplessly.

"No!" Paul cried out.

"This is war," yelled the youth leader shoving the pickaxe into Paul's hands. The deputy guerrilla commander who

59

seemed less agitated whispered something into Paul's ear and the young man nodded. The commander who did not seem to like it beckoned his deputy and talked to him, making firm gestures with his clenched fists. The deputy shrugged his shoulders, shook his head helplessly and moved away. Paul's eyes met with those of his mother and he saw that they were saying something that she could not put into words. The villagers kept on singing. There was nothing to understand.

"No!" Paul cried out again.

The commander let out a single deafening burst of automatic fire into the air and the sound echoed and re-echoed into the humid evening lethargy. The other guerrillas, in various positions around the base, cocked their guns. Now the villagers sang as if they were possessed. Their strident voices left behind haunting echoes floating in the silver light of the moon.

"He is wasting time, Commander," said the youth leader. "He should get on with the business."

"Yes, he should get on with the business," screamed a man from the crowd. The man, another businessman owned a small store next to Paul's father's store.

"Why don't we leave it until tomorrow?" said the deputy commander. "The detachment commander might view it differently."

"There is no time," cut in the section commander.
"But does it have to be an axe?"
"I won't have my deputy disagreeing with me."

The deputy shrugged his shoulders, shook his head and walked away. Paul continued holding the pickaxe looking down at his father but not seeing him. He knew that his father was looking up at him through his puffed and swollen eyes. He also knew that the enormous and tear-laden eyes of his mother were looking at him. The villagers kept singing as if they were possessed. There was absolutely nothing to understand.

"Come on and get over with it!" screamed the youth leader slapping him across the face.

"Please someone help me!" Paul cried, his voice jarred with emotion and tears streaming down his face. The overall commander let out another burst of automatic fire and the villagers, now with voices almost hoarse, sang on.

"Why can't the coward get on with the job?" yelled a female voice from behind the youth leader. "This is not Salisbury!"

"Yes, why can't he get on with the business?" the other businessman screamed standing up. "We are to sit here until day breaks. Jesus! There are more important things to do than sit here all night with a sell-out." He spat on the ground. *"Pamberi nehondo!È"* he yelled and set down.

"But does it have to be an axe?" the deputy commander continued to argue.

"Shut up!" screamed the section commander, his rifle now pointed at him.

The deputy shook his head helplessly and moved away. Behind him, he could hear the vicious cracks as the youth leader hit Paul again and again. He also heard the thud of the butt of the gun as the commander smashed it against Paul's skull. And the jarred voices of the singing villagers – the voices, the villagers.

Then, Paul bent down and began tightening the ropes that bound his father's hands and legs whispering something to himself that he did not know and the tears steadily streaming down his face. All the while, he kept looking away from his father as if he was afraid that he might ask him why he was doing this to him. He could faintly hear his agonised breathing and see the slight trembling in his hands and legs. He stood up and held the pickaxe firmly in both his hands. The sharp blade gleamed in the eerie silver moonlight.

The overall commander shouted: "Lie the sell-out down on his face."

"No!" Paul screamed helplessly. The overall commander let out another burst of fire on the ground in front of Paul and the whole earth shook and trembled. The villagers leapt up and scrambled in all directions but the youths screamed at them to get the hell back and sit down. They got back, sat down and began to sing.

"Why don't we leave it until the detachment commander arrives?" the deputy commander asked again, walking past Paul who was now busy spreading out his father on the ground on his face and stomach whispering to himself something that he did not know and the tears streaming down his face and all the while looking away from him as if he was afraid that he might ask him why he was doing what he was doing and he would not be able to answer and the only thing he could feel was the slight trembling in the man's hands and legs. At last, he stood up and raised the pickaxe with the gleaming blade high above his dazed head and his father groaned and writhed far far down below him and he thought he heard his mother cry. He also thought he heard the deputy guerrilla commander who seemed less agitated plead with his abnormally agitated senior that they should leave the damn thing to the detachment commander but what he heard distinctly was the jarred voice of Amos, the youth leader, and the other businessman screaming at him to get on with the damn business as there was no time. He looked down and the sprawled figure below him lost its shape and its edges got broken and it became a blurred mass. Then he let the pickaxe fall, aiming at the upper end.

"Kill the bloody sell-out!" shouted the youth leader, his eyes filling with gleaming, triumphant tears.

"Please kill him," pleaded the other businessman, his arms and voice shaking with a savage passion.

The fatal explosion that left Paul's mind in blazing flames was not the shattering fury of the pickaxe as it splintered his father's skull but that from the deputy commander's automatic rifle as the bullet crashed through his father's head moments before the pickaxe fell, but for Paul, it was already too late. The axe kept falling again and again and again until he himself, the axe and the blurred mass below him became one huge stain of dark brown blood. And right through, Paul kept crying, pleading with his father not to forgive him but to condemn him forever. The section commander let out a triumphant burst of automatic fire into the air. His deputy walked away wiping away the tears in his eyes with the smoking barrel of his gun, away into the outlying bush. And behind him, the axe kept falling.

The Indian shop owner wrenched the axe away from Paul and pinned him down to the floor screaming at his wife to call the police. Paul kept struggling, crying.

"They made me kill my father and now they want me to kill my mother. Please stop them!"

A plain-clothes police officer flashed his card and pushed his way through the sizeable crowd that had gathered at the entrance of the shop.

"What's the matter?" he asked.

"He is a murderer," said the shop owner. "Get him out of my shop before he murders me or my wife." The officer handcuffed Paul and together with a colleague marched him to the Harare Central Police Station.

"Please help me!" Paul pleaded with the officers. "Don't let them take me. They made me kill my father and now they want me to kill my mother. She is the only one that I have left."

"Who wants to take you?" asked one police officer.

"Those three young men and the woman following us." The police officer, seeing no one behind him, shook his head and marched him on.

Back at home in Mhondoro, when Paul's mother discovered that her son had forgotten his bottle of medicine and knew that even if the last bus to Harare had not gone she did not have the money to use it, she remembered to put on her torn black tennis shoes and began the long walk to Harare, more than sixty kilometres away, whispering to herself, pleading with God and all those gone, especially her husband, to help keep her only child safe and alive as the other one had not returned from the guerrilla war that had freed the country.

Plastic Dreams

She watched them silently as they sauntered into the squatter camp in the heat of the day, hand in hand, their empty bellies aching. Their cracked and unshod feet stirred up the dust as they trudged along. They had met the previous night on the outskirts of Mbare township when each was on his daily round for food. When they met, they had both known that they could have met on any other day over the previous six weeks. If they had met then – or at any other time – they would, as they did now, have thrown their lot in together, just to ease the strain of the colourless days, the endless '*Hapana Basa*: No Work' signs, and the stinging rebuffs from those few distant relatives in the high-density areas. But they also shared silent memories of their bitter, secret pasts. The night they found each other, they had slept peacefully in a gutter.

From a distance, the squatter camp looked even more desolate. It lay squalidly in the afternoon's shimmering heat. Its plastic and cardboard shacks gleamed uneerily in the searing sun. The hovels stood shoulder to shoulder, whimpering their grief like mourners at a funeral. There was not much left save despair and her litter of shrugs.

People were there: men, women and children, all brooding. The women still had a semblance of work to do, washing torn clothes in the dirty water of the Mukuvisi that snaked along the edges of the shanty. Hopeless, they continued to rinse and then dry them on the top of their squalid dwellings. A semblance of pride in cleanliness. They had already walked, as they did every morning, through the industrial areas and the adjacent farms in search of anything remotely usable: firewood, charcoal, bones, waste paper, anything. Later in the afternoon, with the shrilling babies still firmly secured to their backs, they would file out into the market places and sell their wares.

The men lay brooding in the humid shade of their plastic dwellings. They had no more stories to tell. When they still had them, they told them and laughed. Now they survived on one wish. They wished it was Friday. Then, they would hobble to the adjacent Shawasha and Nenyere beer gardens and persuade fifty cent pieces from impatient distant relations, childhood acquaintances or casual sympathisers and buy themselves mugs of Rufaro beer and drink to drown out life. They, too, had been men with homes and a purpose. But that was long ago, long, long ago. What shakily remained were their families: and these too were slowly disintegrating.

Soon, the shacks would not hold anything together. Nothing.

The children brooded, playing in the muddy river-bed. Their bodies were emaciated and their eyes were hollow and glazed. The girls moulded women in high-heeled shoes whilst the boys moulded men driving mercs. They employed themselves with a sad seriousness. They did not go to school; they would never go to school. They were growing up to be thrown out on the streets to help supplement the all time cry for food.

When the two of them, Chaipa and Patrick sauntered into the shanty town, no one gave them a second glance. They were already so much a part of it with their unkempt hair and tattered clothes. They moved through the camp. They wanted a drink of water. The woman stood outside her hovel and surveyed them. She watched them as they approached and crouched in front of her. Her silent eyes followed them as they greeted her. A blade of grass that she was chewing protruded from her mouth.

"Can I help you?" she asked, showing her yellowish teeth. She was tying an elastic band around her untidily plaited hair. Her dress held across one of her shoulders by a thin thread. She wore a single worn-out tennis shoe. Her eyes moved alternately from one to the other as she appraised them. Her gaze finally fixed on Chaipa, her large pained eyes caressing him, as if they were saying... he is old, perhaps older than my current lover and with those eyes he must have experienced terrible things. She surveyed his clothes. She shrugged her shoulders and continued chewing her blade of grass. She looked at his companion. He was just beyond the age of puberty and with that faraway look in the eyes, perhaps he was trying to reconcile his innocent world to the harshness of reality. Well, he would soon know. Yes, he would soon know. She smiled to herself.

"Can you help us with some water?" Chaipa asked clapping his hands.
"What kind?" the woman asked.
"Well. . . ," Chaipa said fidgeting.
"I see," the woman answered, her smile returning.

She crawled into her shack. Inside, a mouldy gloom hung low over an empty five gallon tin, some plates and unwashed pots and a torn folded mat with a single dirty blanket on top of it. She crawled back holding a dirty cup and handed it to Chaipa. He held the cup to his mouth and

67

was attacked by the strong smell of *kachasu*. He gulped the contents expecting to feel the strong, harsh taste of the illicit brew kick at his insides. His spirits fell when he realized that it was after all plain water. He emptied the contents and handed back the cup. She received it, her gaze still fixed on Chaipa.

"Some for my friend too," he said.

As the woman crawled back into her hovel, she thought: there is something funny about them, something I can't yet put my finger on. And then it came to her – friends! Had the older man referred to the youngster as a friend? She shook her head with disbelief. She watched the younger one gulp down the water. She thought: how ridiculous, how can they be real friends? They couldn't possibly be *friends*. With such an age difference, the younger one could be the son of the older man. No, they could not be friends. As the younger one handed her back the empty cup, she received it, shaking her head in disbelief.

"Thank you very much," Chaipa said thrusting out his hand. Her hand was limp and cold. He almost recoiled from its snake-like touch but tried not to show his revulsion.

As the two of them ambled away, their arms locked together, she continued to stare after them, her legs wide apart, one arm akimbo and the other holding the plastic cup. She unconsciously shook her head and said loudly, "I just don't know what to believe." The two of them continued making their way through the shanty town.

The woman resolved that sooner or later, she would know more. She knew that they would still be there the following morning, in a new hovel at the extreme end of the camp. They were not the type that came and left. They came and stayed because there was nowhere else to go. Everyone seemed to come and stay these days. She frowned. Only yesterday, four families had come and pitched their shelters of cardboard and plastic.

She felt a cold shiver run down her spine as she remembered the events of that terrible night. For a moment, she felt again the leaping flames as the hut blazed and she shuddered. She could hear clearly the crackling sound of the flames. But by far the most vivid and painful image was that of her husband and that other woman as they fled from the burning hut. She could see them engulfed in flames, screaming and running round in blind circles as the other villagers tried to douse the fire that burnt them. She had witnessed it all from a hill to the east of the village shortly after setting the hut on fire. She had done it in blind desperation. Her husband, who had taken a second wife, had begun accusing her of all sorts of things: infidelity, stealing and witchcraft. But it was the second wife who finally pushed her over the limit: she had begun accusing her, the first wife, of being responsible for her barren womb. So she had set alight the hut in which they, her husband and his second wife, were sleeping and fled to the city. It was years later that she learnt that they had both survived the fire. She had resolved never to return to the village. She had given up her children. Now as she stood at the edge of the shanty, watching Chaipa and Patrick, two more people running away from their secret pasts, she wished she could return to her village, to her children.

Shivers of uncertainty crept up her spine and tightened round her heart. There was a new rumour that the authorities wanted to set the sprawling shanty ablaze and dump the people on some dry farm near the city. Then what? Where could she go next? She stubbornly resisted her fear and put the rumour out of her mind. Here, no one could think about such eventualities. They had to live for the moment. Tomorrow belonged to nobody. She chuckled mirthlessly as she crawled back into her plastic dream. Before sunset she would invite the two friends for a cup of *kachasu* to destroy whatever defences they thought they had acquired and know them. But already, she was sure about one thing – those men, they were not friends.

69

Not far away to the east, towering buildings stood out against the shimmering sky: grayish blue giants – the city – another world away, another time and other people. And in between, the atmospere held a silent tension, an unresolved issue.

Effortless Tears

We buried my cousin, George Pasi, one bleak windswept afternoon: one of those afternoons that seem fit for nothing but funerals. Almost everyone there knew that George had died of an Aids-related illness but no one mentioned it. What showed was only the fear and uncertainty in people's eyes; beyond that, silence.

Even as we travelled from Harare on that hired bus that morning, every one of us feared that at last Aids had caught up with us. In the beginning, it was a distant, blurred phenomenon which we only came across in the newspapers and on radio and television, something peculiar to homosexuals. Then we began hearing isolated stories of people dying of Aids in far-flung districts. After that came the rumours of sealed wards at Harare and Parirenyatwa, and of other hospitals teeming with people suffering from Aids. But the truth is that it still seemed rather remote and did not seem to have any direct bearing on most of us.

When Aids finally reached Highfield and Zengeza, and started claiming lives in the streets where we lived, that triggered the alarm bells inside our heads. Aids had finally knocked on our doors.

For two months, we had watched George waste away at Harare Hospital. In desperation, his father – just like the rest of us – sceptical of the healing properties of modern medicine, had turned to traditional healers. Somehow, we just could not watch him die. We made futile journeys to all corners of the country while George wasted away. He finally died on our way home from some traditional healer in Mutare.

All the way from Harare to Wedza, the atmosphere was limp. January's scorching sun in the naked sky and the suffocating air intensified into a sense of looming crisis that could not be expressed in words. The rains were already very late and the frequent sight of untilled fields, helplessly confronting an unfulfilling sky created images of seasons that could no longer be understood. The crops that had been planted with the first and only rains of the season had emerged only to fight a relentless war with the sun. Most had wilted and died. The few plants that still survived were struggling in the stifling heat.

Now, as we stood forlornly round the grave, the choir sang an ominous song about death: we named the prophets yielded up to heaven while the refrain repeated: "Can you see your name? Where is your name?"

This eerie question rang again and again in our minds until it became part of one's soul, exposing it to the nakedness of the Mutekedza communal land: land that was overcrowded, old and tired. Interminable rows of huts stretched into the horizon, along winding roads that only seemed to lead to other funerals.

Not far away, a tattered scarecrow from some forgotten season flapped a silent dirge beneath the burning sun.

Lean cattle, their bones sticking out, their ribs moving

painfully under their taut skin, nibbled at something on the dry ground: what it was no one could make out. And around the grave the atmosphere was subdued and silent. Even the once phenomenal Save River, only a stone's throw away to the east, lay silent. This gigantic river, reduced to puddles between heaps of sand seemed to be brooding on its sad predicament. And behind the dying river, Wedza Mountain stared at us with resignation, as if it too had given up trying to understand some of the strange things that were happening.

The preacher told the parable of the Ten Virgins. He warned that when the Lord unexpectedly came and knocked on our door, like the clever five virgins, we should be found ready and waiting to receive Him.

Everyone nodded silently.

George's grandfather mourned the strange doings of this earth. He wished it was him who had been taken away. But then such were the weird ways of witches and wizards that they preferred to pluck the youngest and plumpest – although George had grown thinner than the cattle we could see around us. We listened helplessly as the old man talked and talked until at last he broke down and cried like a small child.

George's father talked of an invisible enemy that had sneaked into our midst and threatened the very core of our existence. He warned us that we should change our ways immediately or die.

He never mentioned the word 'Aids', the acronym A.I.D.S.

George's wife was beyond all weeping. She talked of a need for moral strength during such critical times. She readily admitted that she did not know where such strength could come from: it could be from the people; it could be from those gone beyond; it could be from God. But wherever it was from, she needed it. As if acting upon some invisible signal, people began to cry. We were not weeping for the dead. We were weeping for the living. And behind us, whilst Wedza Mountain gazed at us dejectedly, the Save River was silently dying.

The coffin was slowly lowered into the grave and we filed past throwing in clods of soil. In the casket lay George, reduced to skin and bone. (Most people had refused a last glimpse of him.) During his heyday we had called him Mr Bigstuff because of his fast and flashy style – that was long ago.

As we trudged back to the village, away from the wretched burial area, most of us were trying to decide which memory of George to take back with us: Mr Bigstuff or that thread, that bundle of skin and bones which had died on our way back from some traditional healer in Mutare.

Out there, around the fire, late that Monday evening, all discussion was imbued with an a painful sense of futility, a menacing uncertainty and an overwhelming feeling that we were going nowhere.

Drought.

"Compared to the ravaging drought of 1947, this is child's play," said George's grandfather. "At that time, people survived on grass like cattle," he concluded, looking sceptically up into the deep night sky.

No one helped him take the discussion further.

Politics.

The village chairman of the Party attempted a spirited explanation of the advantages of the government's economic reform programme: "It means a general availability of goods and services and it means higher prices for the people's agricultural produce," he went on, looking up at the dark, cloudless sky. Then, with an inexplicable renewal of optimism peculiar to politicians, he went on to talk of programmes and projects until, somehow, he too was overcome by the general weariness and took refuge in the silence around the dying fire.

"Aren't these religious denominations that are daily sprouting up a sign that the end of the world is coming?" asked George's grandfather.

"No, it's just people out to make a quick buck, nothing else," said George's younger brother.

"Don't you know that the end of the world is foretold in the Scriptures," said the Methodist lay-preacher with sharp urgency. He continued: "All these things," he waved his arms in a large general movement, "are undoubtedly signs of the Second Coming." Everyone looked down and sighed.

And then inevitably, Aids came up. It was a topic that everyone had been making a conscious effort to avoid, but then like everything else, its turn came. Everyone referred to it in indirect terms: that animal, that phantom, that creature, that beast. It was not out of any respect for George. It was out of fear and despair.

"Whatever this scourge is," George's father chuckled, "it has claimed more lives than all my three years in the Imperial Army against Hitler." He chuckled again helplessly.

"It seems as if these endless funerals have taken the place of farming."

"They are lucky, the ones who are still getting decent burials," chipped in someone from out of the dark. "Very soon, there will be no one to bury anybody."

The last glowing ember in the collected heap of ashes grew dimmer and finally died away. George's grandfather asked for an ox-hide drum and began playing it slowly at first and then with gathering ferocity. Something in me snapped.

Then he began to sing. The song told of an unfortunate woman's repeated pregnancies which always ended in miscarriages. I felt trapped.

When at last, the old man, my father, stood up and began to dance, stamping the dry earth with his worn-out

75

car-tyre sandals, I knew there was no escape. I edged George's grandfather away from the drum and began a futile prayer on that moonless night. The throbbing resonance of the drum rose above our voices as we all became part of one great nothingness. Suddenly, I was crying for the first time since George's death. Tears ran from my eyes like rivers in a good season. During those years, most of us firmly believed that the mighty Save River would roll on forever, perhaps until the end of time.

But not now, not any longer.

The Loneliness of a No. 11 Football Player

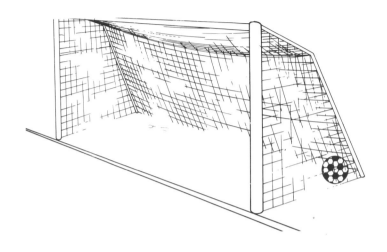

For a whole week, our school could not hide its excitement. Our under-fourteen soccer team had reached the Harare Province DMB[1] finals. The following Friday afternoon, we would be playing the other finalist, a school from Mufakose, at Chibuku Stadium here in Chitungwiza.

The road to the final had been stormy and the most memorable game had taken place during the second round of the knock-outs with one of the nearby schools. I was on the bench as usual, when Tapiwa, our deadly winger intercepted a long inviting pass from one of our full-backs. He connected the pass first time and his rising shot shook the back of the net. We leapt up in jubilation but the referee ruled Tapiwa off-side. Play had to be stopped for more than ten minutes as we swarmed round the referee to try to get him to reverse his 'biased' decision. With the scoreline deadlocked at 1 - 1, we thought we had snatched the lead and the game. Anyway, our coach, Mr Soko, urged our boys to resume play and within a minute,

---

[1] Dairy Marketing Board

Tapiwa was on target again. Oh God, Tapiwa, what could we do without you?

But all this is beside the point. I am not telling the story of how our under-fourteen team got to the DMB final. No! I am telling my own painful story. By the way, my name is Alois Nyemba and I am in Grade 7. I have one big heartache, one big disappointment – the Number 11 jersey. Last year when I was playing in the school's 'B' team, I was certain that next year, this year, I would be wearing the Number 11 jersey in the 'A' team. Who else besides me could wear it after the departure of Caleb, who was then in Grade 7? But unfortunately, things did not turn out that way.

Hardly a week after school opened at the beginning of the year, along comes this tall, thin chap. They put him in our class. I did not take any particular notice of him. I doubt if anybody did. I did not even bother to find out much about him. A rather lanky morose fellow, he gave me the discouraging impression of someone perpetually about to cry. But what I did not know was that he had a deadly left foot and that, in the end, he would rob me of the Number 11 jersey.

What made me even more bitter and angry was his natural grace and ease with the ball. He did not seem to exert *any* effort. Things seemed to just happen for him: the way he controlled the ball, the way he dribbled, the way he laid his passes, and the way he shot his goals! He, Tapiwa, was so good that I was left seething with jealousy. The other painful thing I had to bear lay in Mr Soko's eyes, for these shone with excitement each time Tapiwa had the ball. I sometimes wondered why they did not pop out of their sockets! Mr Soko would even ask Tapiwa to demonstrate various new techniques to us. In a very short time, it was clear that Mr Soko regarded Tapiwa as the backbone of our team. And the person who suffered most was poor me.

At first Mr Soko did not want to reveal that my position

in the team was doomed. He flattered me with statements about what a great player I promised to be. His words, although they were obviously untrue, soothed me. At practice I worked flat out. Each morning, I ran ten laps around the school ground and I forced my father to buy me a leather football. But somewhere inside me, I knew that I would never possess the wizardry of Tapiwa. And one unhappy afternoon during practice, Mr Soko confirmed my fears. I was thrown back into the 'B' team. I cannot say with conviction that I began to hate Tapiwa, but the sight of him made me feel uncomfortable and each time our eyes met, my throat would tighten and my heart would beat very fast. I do not know what that was all about.

But what made Tapiwa the talk of the whole school – in fact he became a hero – was when we began the knock-out matches for the DMB trophy. In the opening two matches, Tapiwa slammed an incredible five goals. With Tapiwa in such amazing form, I could not understand why Mr Soko kept me on the bench wearing the Number 12 jersey. The sky-blue uniform only made me more acutely aware of my limitations. I felt no pride in wearing that uniform, no happiness, only an inexplicable emptiness. On the one hand, there was Tapiwa, who was everything I wanted to be, with everyone, especially the girls, chanting his name around the football field. (There were moments when I could almost swear I heard Rudo's lovely voice high above others.) And yet there was poor me, sitting like a reject on the bench with Mr Soko and two other substitutes. It seemed illogical for the people who liked Tapiwa to like me. For how could they like me when I was the exact opposite of all that Tapiwa was? If Mr Soko had not implored me to wear the Number 12 jersey and sit with him on that wretched bench, I would not have done so. No: to be spiked by the pain of people chanting Tapiwa's name, no! I would not only have stopped coming to watch the games, I would have stopped training altogether. But Mr Soko implored me to continue.

However, something I had not expected happened during

training practice two days before that crucial final. Tapiwa sprained his ankle! At first, Mr Soko, indeed all of us, thought that it was a mild sprain which would heal overnight, but when Tapiwa failed to come to Assembly the following morning, we began to worry. Even as Mr Soko took us for oral arithmetic after Assembly, I could see slowly increasing panic in his eyes. Tapiwa had still not arrived. Indeed, he only managed to limp in just before break with his clearly swollen leg heavily bandaged. It seemed increasingly likely that Tapiwa would not play in the final the following day. The news of this frightening possibility spread through the school like a deadly virus and everyone became hysterical. Small Grade 1 pupils came and peeped through our classroom window during break while a cluster of anxious girls (including Rudo) hovered around Tapiwa to wish him a miraculous recovery. In the afternoon, the headmaster and Mr Soko rushed Tapiwa into town to see a specialist. The desperation to have Tapiwa play in the final gripped the whole school. I watched all these goings-on as dispassionately as possible. There was no place in the fuss for me.

They brought him back from town late that afternoon and just from their demeanour, we could see it was all over. The headmaster walked with a heavy, defeated limp and Mr Soko's face was ashen. Then Mr Soko broke the sad news. "The doctor said it might take another three to four days before the sprain heals." There was a stunned silence. "Who will replace him?" someone groaned. At least it seemed like a groan. Mr Soko rubbed his palms together and looked at me.

"But it's the final!" someone else exclaimed.
"We have no choice boys," Mr Soko said dejectedly.
"But that goose is in disastrous form," someone said, looking pointedly at me.

The sudden realization that I was the focus of attention, negative attention, made me panic. Sweat leaked from my body. How could it not with everyone's accusing finger pointing at me? I began to disintegrate. Even as Mr Soko took us through our exercises, as I was not on form.

On our way home I kept to myself. I could hear Amos, our centre back, lamenting loudly: "Guys, we are done for. With that clown as our winger we are as good as ten." My heart wanted to crack but I held it firmly together although tears welled up in my eyes. I continued walking alone in front of them. Everyone was against me. It seemed as if I was responsible for Tapiwa's misfortune.

At home that evening, I did not have the appetite to eat. Surprised by my listless mood, my mother asked whether anything was wrong. I lied and told her that I had a slight headache. That night I slept, but I had serious nightmares which left me soaked with sweat. In the first, I was drowning in a deep, dark pool. A pole that Rudo was holding out to me was too short by a few centimetres. My struggle to grab it went on and on with both Rudo and me desperately crying out and just as I was to about to sink, I jumped out of bed.

"What ever is the matter, Alois? You were shouting in your sleep?" It was my father standing by my bedside. "It must have been a nightmare," he said. "Try to calm down and get back to sleep." I went back to sleep and within a short time, I was in the throes of yet another nightmare. We were now playing the crucial match, a tough match indeed. One of our strikers was fouled in the penalty box and we were awarded a penalty. They all asked me to take it but I refused. It was a trap. Since we were trailing 1 - 0, I knew they wanted to blame me for our impending defeat. No, I would not take the penalty. But even Mr Soko seemed to be part of the conspiracy. He intervened and told me to do so. I blasted the ball over the bar! And then everyone started to attack me, crush me. I could hardly breathe. I was dying. I woke up violently. It was then that I made a desperate decision. I would refuse to play in the final on the following day.

The following day, Tapiwa came to school without the bandage but from the way he walked, there was no doubt that he was in pain. Everyone, especially the girls, clustered around him, examining his ankle and offering to massage it. I tried to convince myself that he was not enjoying it – after all I would have done – and that what I was seeing on his face was anguish. I watched all this hoo-ha from a distance, as if I was not concerned. My only satisfaction was the secret knowledge that I would refuse to play at the last minute.

We did not learn much that day. The school dismissed at break to give us enough time to walk to Chibuku stadium some four kilometres away. The match was scheduled to kick-off at two o'clock that afternoon. As the seconds slowly ticked towards the hour, my loneliness became more acute. The closer it came to two, the more people distanced themselves from me. No one wanted to talk with me. Somehow all the excitement that had gripped the school for a whole week had vanished. In its place the abstract finger of cold, silent, angry tension pointed accusingly at me. I was the black sheep of the school, I was the one responsible for its misfortunes. I was absolutely convinced that the only recourse open to me was to refuse to play in the final. As far as I was concerned, that decision was a matter of life or death. I would tell Mr Soko of my decision in the changing room, just before kick-off.

Our school arrived at the stadium to a thunderous reception from the unbelievably large crowd that had come to cheer us on to victory. The school from Mufakose had already arrived. A small group of their supporters were singing and beating drums in one corner of the grandstand. Although we were not playing at our school, we were home. That increased the pressure on our team. We had to win, or let everyone here down. Our victory would be a victory for the whole of Chitungwiza. The VIPs in the special enclosure included several councillors, headmasters from all the schools in the area and some local businessmen. Our school had to win. But secretly I knew that I would not play in the crucial match.

When we got to the changing room all the muffled talk about the match and me had died away. The formidable seriousness of the game, now only a few minutes away, had struck home. But perhaps I was wrong. Perhaps it was my worthless presence in the team that had killed everyone's spirit. Mr Soko, smoking cigarette after cigarette, started giving out the jerseys. My hands were trembling. Now that the time had come, I steeled myself to make my refusal. He held out the Number 11 jersey to me but I kept my head down.

"Come on, boy, time is running out," he shouted. I kept my head down.

"Hey, Alois, what's got into you?" he asked anxiously, licking his lips. My eyes filled and huge tears fell to the floor. He noticed. "Come on, my boy, what's wrong with you now?" Everyone was looking at us. Suddenly, something very heavy settled in my chest. I could not breathe; I was dying. Tears fell from my eyes and I began to sob. Mr Soko started patting me on the shoulder and I felt immensely relieved. "Boy, you are going to be the star," he said. Somehow, I was no longer afraid. I took the jersey and wore it.

Our team got onto the pitch for the brief warm-up before the game. There was deafening applause from the terraces. Our sky-blue uniform shone triumphantly in the sun. We formed a circle around the centre and waved to the crowds. The stadium exploded. Yes, the crowd was with us. Mr Soko's words kept ringing in my mind. I was no longer afraid.

The game started at a very fast pace and before anyone from our team had settled into the rhythm, three players from Mufakose exchanged quick passes and a fierce shot crashed against the cross-bar, with our goalkeeper watching helplessly. A cold chill ran down my spine and my heart started beating very fast. We had not fully recovered from that shock when again, one of the Mufakose players dispossessed us and laid a beautiful pass to their Number 9. Our goalkeeper dived out at full stretch, just got his hand on the scorching shot and pushed it out for a corner. The crowd started shouting at us to get the hell organized. I stole a furtive glance at Mr Soko. His hunched figure was poised on the bench like a question mark, holding his massive head in this hands. Things had started very badly. I kept to the touch-line. Mr Soko had always instructed me to keep to the touch-line. Until then, I had not touched the ball but I could swear I was not the only one.

Then we began to settle down. One of our half-backs intercepted a square pass from Mufakose, dribbled his way past one person and laid a neat pass on to one midfielder. The midfielder picked the ball up, made a dazzling solo run across the field and flicked a looping ball at the goal. The confused goalkeeper punched it but it was one of the defenders who cleared it from the line. I still had not touched the ball and I began to feel I must be the only one in this position. Something inside me slowly began to crack. But still, I kept to the touch-line.

Our team came under heavy pressure again as Mufakose mounted dangerous raid after dangerous raid. They were virtually camped in our half of the field and when their goal finally came, it was long overdue. It was their central defender who fired home at point-blank range. Perhaps it was that score which exposed my complete uselessness in the game. I uneasily kept to the touch-line. The crowd started jeering at me to get the hell into the game and help the others. I started to sweat. And then it happened. In a frantic effort to clear the ball, one of our defenders booted out a long ball that found me alone without a single Mufakose defender near me, near the centre circle. I did not know what to do. In a hasty and clumsy attempt to control the ball I tripped and fell down. The whole stadium exploded into a rumbling 'boo'. My heart burst and began to bleed. I tried to pick myself up but all my joints had turned to jelly. I lay there prostrate on the ground, with the hundreds of jeering voices and contorted faces whirling around and around in my foggy mind. Riding high above this wave of booing voices was Rudo's, very clear in its vehement condemnation. By the time I finally rose, my whole world had disintegrated. I had sold out my team on one of the few chances that had fallen its way. The referee blew for half-time.

My team-mates started trotting to Mr Soko for the usual half-time pep talk. From the way they ran, I could see that they felt very free; their consciences were clear. None of them was to blame. I trudged behind them, kicking a loose piece of newspaper, silently wishing that I would never arrive in the semi-circle that the others had formed around Mr Soko. *"Iwe Alois kurumidza mheni,"*[2] shouted Tapiwa behind Mr Soko. He was wearing the Number 14 jersey. A large crowd had formed around the players to chip in their advice. The girls were also there, including Rudo. I could see her in my mind's eye pulling faces behind my back. My heart ached.

Surprisingly it was Mr Soko who came to my rescue. Everyone was calling for my blood. At one point, the pep talk became so emotional that some players started shaking their fists in my face. What seemed to irritate everyone was not only that I had squandered a golden opportunity to level the score-line but that I was a virtual spectator in the game. Everyone cried out for my substitution. Mr Soko was in a dilemma. There was no one who could play my position. George, our team captain, came out with a brilliant idea. Why not shift Stanley from Number 7 to 11 and bring in Tito? Mr Soko shook his head thoughtfully. I could not understand why he disagreed with the strategy. I just looked on helplessly as everyone argued over my fate. Then the referee blew for resumption of play. My case had not been resolved.

[2] Get a move on, Alois!

The second half began at a brisk pace with our team launching frantic raids in search of an equaliser. But the Mufakose side absorbed all the pressure, replying with sporadic dangerous counter-raids. I did not keep to the touch-line any more. It was on one of those Mufakose counter-raids that I nearly caused another disaster. A Mufakose winger flighted a high ball from near the corner flagpost into the box. I was there in the box. As the high ball descended ominously towards me, I did not know what to do. Should I head it or boot it? There was not enough time to decide. As a result, I tried to do both at the same time. The ball deflected off my shoulder and crashed against one of the goal posts before our goalkeeper collected it safely. I had almost given Mufakose an own-goal! The stadium shook with furious jeers. Everyone was clamouring for my immediate removal from the team. There was panic on our bench. Through the corner of my eye I could see Tapiwa warming up, limping up and down the touch line. The girls started chanting his name with the boys clapping their hands. I could also see the headmaster whispering something into Mr Soko's ear. The situation had become desperate. About twenty minutes of play remained.

I don't know who initiated the move but what I remember clearly was Nyika, one of our midfielders, beating clean three players from Mufakose. He laid a neat pass to Chamu, another of our midfielders, who in turn beat two Mufakose players and passed the ball on to me just outside the penalty box. I dashed for the ball, tightly marked by two defenders and a third coming straight on at me. It was an impossible position. There was only one thing that I wanted to do – to lay my foot on the ball. With an astonishing heave, I swung my left foot towards the ball. The last thing I heard was the ominous crunch of the collision as the four of us somersaulted into a painful pile, each writhing in agony. Then I briefly passed out.

As I came to I realized I was being carried shoulder-high

and the pitch was overrun by a flood of chanting people. What had happened? I could see Mr Soko waving his white handkerchief jubilantly. He only did that when our team had scored. Had our team scored? Who had scored? Amidst this sea of excited people, the referee was desperately ordering everyone out of the pitch for the match to resume. Then they put me down. Rudo appeared from nowhere and rubbed the sweat off my face with her wool-soft hand. "Aren't you hurt, ALOIS? The eye is swollen slightly," she said feeling it. I felt a tickling sensation ripple through my body. I had never felt so good. "That was a beautiful score, Alois," she said, her gentle eyes avoiding mine. (They told me later that it was a spectacular shot that rose and curved leaving the goalkeeper diving the other way. Mr Soko vowed that in his entire twenty years as a football coach, he had never witnessed such a tantalising goal.)

Play resumed some ten minutes later with only about five minutes of play left and the scores now deadlocked at 1 - 1. I had got over the tumultuous confusion of being the hero of a goal that I neither saw nor could describe. How could I be expected to enjoy the glory of a goal that happened seemingly on its own? I felt guilty before the wildly chanting crowd. My thoughts were still tangled in this maze of emotion when again something incredible happened. I remember very clearly Stanley taking a corner and the high ball coming and coming but I do not recall what they told me later. They told me that I out-jumped the entire Mufakose defence and banged in a flashing header past the mesmerized goalkeeper. We had snatched the lead! The stadium exploded, and not even the referee could do anything about it. They carried me round and round the football pitch chanting a song: "Alois is our lion. Alois is our lion. Alois is our lion." I took all this in, in a dazed fashion.

By the time play finally resumed, we had already won the game. And when the referee blew for full time, it was only formality. They carried me all the way to the grandstand where I dreamily received the floating trophy and a cheque of $500.00. I almost cried. They also carried me all the way back to school chanting my name and, as they did so, my inner turmoil intensified. I was a fake, a fraud thriving on two accidental goals that I had scored with my eyes closed. Then the girls said they also wanted to carry me.

As four big girls prepared to lift me up, Rudo rubbed off the sweat from my face with her handkerchief, her eyes avoiding mine. My heart began to throb wildly and the chanting voices began to recede. I could not see although my eyes were wide open. Then Rudo appeared and filled my whole mind. To hell with the game. To hell with the trophy and all this fake glory. To hell with the Number 11 jersey. I no longer felt lonely.

Circles

We sat silent, waiting for the chairman. Inside, we were seething with fury. We had had enough of him. He was not even going to chair this hastily called meeting – the vice-chairman, Comrade Mguza, would do so. The chairman's presence was only required as a formality. Everyone was fed up with his style of leadership. Every member of our co-operative had resolved that this would be an historic meeting. And so we sat with the women on one side and the men on the other.

Not far from where we sat stood the blue tractor, the cause of all the controversy. We had bought it with our hard-earned money. Each one of the fifty of our co-operative members had contributed $200. We had bought it to alleviate the draught power shortage after the crippling drought. Of the $10 000 that we had already paid back, there still remained owing the balance of $20 000. To offset this balance, we had planted twenty hectares of cotton in what we called our collective field where we all worked once a week. Of course we expected to get more than the outstanding $20 000, but we had plans to buy another tractor with the surplus.

But now, here we were, bogged right down at the beginning with the chairman treating the tractor as if it were his own personal property and drawing up a ploughing programme which favoured his relatives and friends. The season's late rains were already in their fourth week, yet most of us, who were neither his relatives nor his friends, had not even planted a seed under the ground. We sat angrily, waiting for the chairman.

He came in silently and seemed shocked for a moment by the gathering but he discreetly suppressed his bewilderment. He sat down next to the secretary, Comrade Manonga, who was busy fumbling for his notebook. There was a charged silence.

Then the vice-chairman stood up and raised his clenched fist: "Forward with co-operation!" he cajoled.

"Pamberi!" we echoed back.

"Down with individualism!"

"Down!"

"Down with nepotism!"

"Down!"

He took off his slouch hat. "Comrades, pardon us for this hastily called meeting," he said more to the chairman than to us. "We had to call for it to crush the worm that is eating away at our co-operative." He looked at the chairman. The chairman looked down, making patterns on the wet ground with the toes of his bare feet. The secretary wrote furiously in his notebook.

"This co-operative belongs to us," shouted Mudhara Dore from the floor.

"Order!" said the vice-chairman calmly. "I am the chairman."

"You are *not* the chairman," retorted Mudhara Dore stamping his foot on the ground.

"Of course I am not *the* chairman," the vice-chairman said exasperated, "but I am the chairman of this meeting!" He threw his arms into the air and sighed.

"Please, comrades, let's get on with the meeting," said the secretary. There was a brief silence. The chairman was still looking down drawing patterns on the ground with the toes of his bare feet. The vice-chairman cleared his throat.

"Because of the serious mismanagement of the chairman's handling of the tractor, the people here call for his immediate dismissal. After all, we chose him."

"I second the motion!" I heard myself shouting, even to my surprise.

"But no one has told him the reasons yet," said the secretary. The vice-chairman frowned. The chairman kept looking down.

"Which of us doesn't know of the gross irregularities besetting our co-op because of him?" the vice-chairman asked, pointing his finger at the chairman. "Do we need to repeat them? No, we do not!"

"But he also has to say something, if only for the record," the secretary insisted.

Somehow, I found myself standing up and pointing at the chairman. "He has thrown out, through his own window, the code of rules that bind our co-operative. He thinks that by being chairman he has risen above everyone of us. We are all equal in this co-op!" Everyone was listening. The room was quiet. "Why should I go and kneel before him for a tractor over which I have an equal claim?"

The members clapped wildly. The secretary wrote furiously in his notebook. The vice-chairman looked at me, mesmerized. The chairman continued to look down and draw patterns on the ground with the toes of his bare feet. I continued, "The rules of this co-op are above everyone of us. They are sacred. They are our bible. For example, we chose a driver for the tractor – Charles." I looked at Charles. Everyone followed my eyes. "But what did our honourable chairman do?" I waited for someone to answer.

"He chose his own," shouted Mudhara Dore.

"And who is that?" I asked again. I was beginning to enjoy myself.

"His son Joshua!" the crowd roared. I motioned everyone to silence. There was an abrupt silence. The vice-chairman continued looking at me as if he was seeing me for the first time.

"Comrades, the time has come for us to take positive and decisive action." I sat down. The clapping, whistling and ululation that followed took more that three minutes to stop. When finally the vice-chairman brought the small house to order, he said, "The meeting has resolved that the chairman be replaced. Nominations?"

"But there has to be a vote of no confidence first," appealed the secretary.

"Progress! He is taking us back," someone shouted from the floor.

"I am sorry if I appear to be supporting the chairman, but I think we have to run our affairs properly. If I were asked for my suggestion I would say let us choose a committee responsible for managing the tractor. Why indeed dismiss the chairman? We are learning aren't we?"

"What's got into the head of the secretary?" Mai Maswera asked, looking curiously at him. The secretary swallowed and sat down quickly before resuming writing.

"I have always warned you to be careful when making these elections. Some people are wolves in sheeps' clothing," said Amai Moyo. The secretary swallowed again and flicked through the pages of his notebook.

"Nominations please," said the vice-chairman.

For the first time, the chairman raised his head and lifted his hand to say something. The vice-chairman ignored him. "How many names? I think two will do," he answered himself. "Are you raising your hand, Amai Mguza? Yes please," he said picking on his wife. The startled woman stood up and looked around confusedly. "Was I raising my hand?" she asked unsurely. "Anyway I choose Comrade Murove," she said looking at me. The vice-chairman swallowed and his jaw dropped. The chairman kept raising his hand.

"Any seconder?" the vice-chairman asked ignoring the chairman. More than a dozen hands flung into the air. "Second nomination?" the vice-chairman asked hesitantly. No one raised their hands. "Second nomination," the vice-chairman asked, his voice sharp and urgent.

"Let Comrade Murove stand unopposed," Amai Moyo said. The chairman still had his hand up. The vice-chairman looked at him uncertainly and his lips began to tremble.

"*Pamberi na* Comrade Murove!" someone shouted from the crowd.

"*Pamberi!*" everyone answered in a chorus. The deafening response echoed round and round in my mind. My vision became blurred as I majestically rose and walked to assume my newly acquired role. The people cheered. Someone started singing a song that had my name in it. I dreamily started clapping my hands. Everyone followed suit. I raised my hands and the people fell silent.

"*Pamberi nemushandirapamwe!*"[1] I said dreamily.
"*Pamberi!*" they responded.
"*Pamberi na*chairman!" I said
"*Pamberi!*" they chorused.

"From now on, we will give Kumboyedzawo Co-operative a new image, a new thrust, a new direction. Comrade vice-chairman, start drawing up tomorrow's ploughing programme, beginning with those who have never had the tractor in their fields." The people became frenzied as the vice-chairman wrote their names down. I walked over

[1] Forward with the co-operative

93

to the tractor and started stroking it gently. Charles, the driver, came to me.

"Since the vice-chairman is drawing up tomorrow's programme, what will I do this afternoon?" he asked.

I looked over the low brushline and my eyes fell on my unploughed piece of land. The back of my ears began to itch. Charles kept looking at me and I looked across at the receding hunched figure of the ex-chairman silently walking away and then back again at my unploughed piece of land. Charles shrugged his shoulders.

"When do you want me to start on it, Comrade Chairman?"

I rubbed my moist palms together, walked limply past the baffled vice-chairman, behind the receding hunched figure of the ex-chairman, towards nowhere.

Behind me I could hear the sputtering sound of the tractor as Charles drove towards my piece of land. I half-turned to call to him to stop but a sense of acute hopelessness overcame me. I walked away faster, afraid to see the people stop what they were doing and stare at me in bewilderment. A short distance ahead of me, the ex-chairman stopped and waited, as if to welcome me.

Patches

When the little boy, Tonderai, finally left the village and joined his mother and step-father at the farm near Makwiro, he quickly became friends with the silent railway line that passed through the farm at the edge of the compound in front of the small farm store. Each day, long after the trains had thundered past, the little boy would be standing on the veranda of the small store, gazing at the twin steel lines and their smooth shining silver tops. The lines, lying side by side but never touching, stretched silently into the unknown. There was a loneliness about them, a sad desolation, a sense of predicament for they seemed to be permanently whispering to each other. Where did the lines end? the little boy wondered. Hope, or rather a future, seemed to lie there.

As each day passed and as more and more trains thundered past, the little boy felt a growing empathy with the railway line. He and the silent line seemed to share the silence together. Where did the line end? Perhaps there was a future there.

During the evenings, the little boy would sit alone in the darkness on the veranda of the small farm store and cry silently as he watched the trains thunder past. One day his step-brother, Hamidhu, told on him and his step-father caught him weeping as he watched the railway line.

"Why are you crying?" the man asked angrily. The little boy wiped the tears off his face and looked away. "You are mad!" he shouted and walked away to demand that his four children shun this crazy, illegitimate child who cried for nothing. The little boy could not understand his step-father's anger and sadly watched the mysterious line.

At night, especially during the weekend, the thundering noise of the trains would be drowned by the sobbing of the little boy's mother after his step-father had beaten her. Then Tonderai's mind would drift towards the two steel lines that, although only a few centimetres apart, never touched and he would sense a kind of togetherness, a strange loneliness.

During the day, the little boy would see his step-brothers throw careless talk at each other just as they threw stones on their way back from the farm school and he would marvel at their navy blue uniforms against his own torn and patched shirt and pair of shorts.It was Hamidhu who nicknamed him Patches, and then everyone started to call him Patches including his step-father. His mother cried but her helplessness only drew him closer to the railway line and the strong, thundering trains and then he would walk aimlessly on the wooden slippers between the twin lines feeling a strange sense of security and comfort.

One hot afternoon, as he sat on the veranda of the small farm store with the storekeeper, Mrs Phili, who was also the wife of the farm foreman, a goods train roared by. The open country was dry and the sky laden with endless ridges of drifting, dry season clouds. One particularly fat cloud at the edge of the sky seemed to be racing the train. Tonderai watched the race in fascination. As the cloud and the goods train ran shoulder to shoulder, so the cloud seemed to get the better of the train. Then they both disappeared over the horizon. The little boy hoped the train had won.

"Where does the railway line end?" he asked the foreman's wife.

The woman shot him a suspicious glance. "It goes on and on. Why?"

"On and on and on?"

"Until it gets to Harare. Why?"

"And beyond Harare?"

"There are other lines, many of them."

"And where do those end?"

"They keep on going and going but that's not important. What is important is that they all lead to Harare. Every line leads to Harare."

"All lines?"

"Yes, all lines. The goods train that has just passed is coming from Harare and is going wherever it is going only to return to Harare. It belongs to Harare. Many things belong to Harare."

"Have you ever been there?"

She slowly put away her knitting and her eyes lit up and her face began to glow. "Yes," she whispered dreamily. "I've been there. I've seen Harare's bright lights."

"Do you want to go back there again?"

She quickly picked up her knitting, the lights in her eyes disappeared and the smile on her face ran away. "It is not possible now. It's not possible."

"I'd like to go there."

"It can be dangerous. It's no place for children, or even

for grown-ups. That's where I met the foreman," she frowned and looked away. "It can be very frustrating." She paused. "Children who go there without their parents live on the streets and sleep on the streets. They eat from garbage cans and spend their days guarding people's cars. It's not a good place for children."

"But they are happy," he said with a sudden, sharp, questioning urgency. "Besides, my father is somewhere there."

The woman looked at him and then away. "Your mother will not allow that," she said as if in answer to his unspoken words.

During the afternoons as the little boy sat on the veranda of the small store watching the trains and wondering about Harare, he would see Sixpence, the tractor driver, drive his machine to the store, buy the wife of the foreman a bottle of Coca Cola and a packet of Lemon Creams and then hug her before driving quickly back to the fields. And in the store, the wife of the foreman would increase the volume of the cassette player and with eyes lit up and face glowing, she would begin to dance, moving her waist sideways, backwards and forwards and the little boy would look up the railway line and wonder what Harare was like. The things that the wife of the foreman sometimes did could only belong to Harare. And once in a while, when she was happy, she would give him a biscuit or even leave him her half-finished bottle of Coca Cola.

Things changed dramatically when the elder brother of his step-father arrived from Harare. The man had pitch black dyed hair and wore blue jeans and high-heeled shoes. Then his mother and step-father quarrelled all night and the little boy could hear his name being mentioned even above the vibrating noise of the passing trains. Later still that night, the little boy watched the elder brother of his step-father open his travelling bag in the dull candlelight and saw inside the biggest bunch of keys that he had ever seen, two gleaming knives and a wad of twenty dollar notes. Then the man turned and looked at him with cold, bloodshot eyes, the little boy quickly looked away and the man made a sinister noise in his throat.

The following day, the little boy saw the man from Harare come to the store and talk with the wife of the foreman. They talked and talked until at last they began to laugh. The driver of the tractor came and left immediately without buying the wife of the foreman anything. The wife of the foreman and the elder brother of the little boy's step-father continued to laugh carelessly, pointing their fingers at the man on top of the moving tractor. The elder brother of the little boy's step-father later bought the wife of the foreman a bottle of Coca Cola and a packet of Lemon Creams and the woman's eyes lit up and her face glowed like the lights of Harare and the railway line shone in the sun.

When, the following morning, the wife of the foreman did not open the store, the little boy wondered what had happened as he gazed at the clean, straight railway line. And when in the afternoon he overheard his step-brother say that the wife of the foreman had disappeared from the compound, the little boy knew that she had fled to Harare with the elder brother of his step-father who had returned to Harare very early that morning, and a painful loneliness overwhelmed him. He sat all afternoon on the veranda of the closed store and the foreman came again and again to peer into the store through the window, as if he expected to see his wife inside; and when the sun went down and the land was covered in a cold darkness and the railway line was cold to touch, the little boy felt very alone. Occasionally, an engine driver would blow the sharp piercing horn of his train down the line that stretched on and on into the darkness. Some trains were going to

Harare and those that were not going were coming from Harare only to go back there again.

Tonderai stood up, left the compound and walked over to the railway line. He looked searchingly up the tracks that gleamed in the silver light of the moon until for a moment he thought he saw the glowing yellow lights of Harare in the night sky and a hunger for the city enveloped him. Then he knew that he would jump into the wagon of a goods train and go to Harare, go away from his pain and emptiness, towards hope and the end of the line.

The (Wo)man in the Mirror

When the heavy downpour that had laid siege to the night finally ceased, when the spent clouds that had shut out the sky finally allowed a little limp sunshine to wash away the hanging mist, when the township, Kambuzuma, awoke at last, Alfred Ndoro found himself thinking about his home and family. Each time such thoughts stole up on him, they unsettled him and he would flee to the township beerhall to hide in the milling crowds, the blaring music from the jukebox and the long mugs of opaque beer. But as he left the room, he caught sight of his reflection in the wardrobe mirror and stopped. He looked hard at his squat nose, smouldering eyes and greying beard, then shrugging his shoulders, he left the room. He thought he looked strange.

As if to distance himself from his uncomfortable thoughts, he walked briskly along the path that separated Section Three from Section Two. It was thick with weeds and waves of swaying grass – a path that evoked memories of one's youth if, like Alfred, one had grown up in the country. He walked across the ugly gully filled with mud and red sludge after the heavy rains and on past the first row of houses in Section Two, past the high fence of the government primary school, past the shopping centre, the open market and on towards the beerhall. It was at the small drift that he caught up with the two women.

What shocked him about them was not that they were talking about him – although he did not know them – but just how much they knew about him, especially the plump one with the careless laughter.

She laughed. "When everything has been said, he is a sorry figure who seems to have lost control of his life." She laughed again. "Would you by any chance know him?" she asked her companion.

"I'm not quite sure," the woman said. "There are so many men lodging at VaChida's house."

"How about you, *mukuwasha*. Do you know this man, Alfred Ndoro?" the plump one asked Alfred. A cold shiver ran down his spine as he replied in the negative. The plump one continued, "I have seen him from a distance, but although I have never talked with him, I'm sure I would know him if I saw him. Did you know that he has just divorced his fourth wife?"

"Fourth!" responded the other woman. And then as if he were a cheap, popular novel, the woman with the careless laughter began flipping through the torn, dirty pages of his life.

"That man is lost and beyond rescue," she said. "Whilst his children wander from relative to relative like stray cattle, he is locked into a breathless love affair with some divorcee in Kuwadzana who is almost the age of his mother. That's where all his money is going. What a fool," she said emotionally. Alfred swallowed.

"The dilemma that straddles their home is a big one," said the other woman.

"Those who know say that the spirit of an avenging woman sits cross-legged in the middle of their home and

102

all efforts to appease her have failed. Unless they give her what she wants, their home will remain one for men alone and no woman will ever stay in there. She is the only woman who will stay in that place."

"Where do they say she came from and what does she want that seems so difficult to provide?" the other woman asked. Alfred swallowed as he walked between the two. Could it be true that neither of them recognized him?

"Those who know say she was from Masvingo and was married to one of the boys in the family. He died in a mine accident and then their problems started. Those left behind wanted to take her over but she refused them. Then at the height of the liberation war she was killed, allegedly for being a witch. Those who know say that this man Alfred was instrumental in her death."

"Really!" exclaimed the other woman. Alfred began to sweat.

"And now what she wants is a husband. She wants to be given officially to someone as 'the' wife and her demand has torn the family apart."

"But who on earth would want to get married to a dead person?"

"This doesn't seem to matter as far as the other members of the family are concerned," said the one with the careless laughter. "They say the person who planned her death must face the consequences."

"So that leaves us with poor Alfred?"

"Yes of course," replied the plump woman. Alfred unconsciously opened his mouth to protest but not a word came out and the woman with the careless laughter continued her onslaught. "He once took refuge in the Johanne Masowe Apostolic Faith Sect. In fact he became a renowned faith healer and everything seemed to improve until the sect gave him a wife." Again Alfred opened his mouth to protest, but again he said nothing, so the plump woman continued. "It is alleged that the dead woman sought him out and so then he turned to traditional healers and fortune tellers."

"Why doesn't he just accept her as his wife . . . he would at least find some peace?"

"Get married to a dead person? You can't be serious Mai Nyasha? Do you know what you've just said?"

"Well, perhaps I thought that rather than spend one's life running away from trouble, he had better just face up to it?"

"And live with a dead woman? And sleep with her?" A cold shiver ran down Alfred's back and he tried to find the voice to protest, to give his own version of events, but getting nowhere he simply shrugged his shoulders helplessly.The plump woman laughed carelessly before continuing. "Now he is deep in witchcraft. He has met practically every *n'anga* in and around town. Some even claim to have met him as far afield as Chipinge as he tries to turn this woman away towards other members of his family. After all, who would sit back and let someone do what they like in a case like this? His family have united against him, so they will always drive the woman back."

"That's not true!" Alfred heard himself exclaim loudly.

"Did you say something?" the woman with the careless laughter asked.

"No, yes, I meant. . . I said we have a similar case in our village. Isn't it strange how these things can often be so alike?" he said.

The plump one laughed carelessly before continuing. "The last time he was home several years ago, those who know say he was almost axed to death by one of his brothers. They don't want to see him. It is said the whole family pursued him with axes and spears and he only survived by taking refuge in a neighbouring village." Alfred's heart missed a beat.

"You seem very well informed, Mai Rudo," the other woman said.

"He is now not much more than a moving bag of snuff," the plump one said, laughing carelessly. Alfred's hand dropped to his side as he felt furtively for the duiker horn snuff container in his jacket pocket. She continued, "Anyway there is nothing else worth talking about in his room: there is nothing there except metres and metres of red, black and white cloth that he uses to cover the walls and wear." Again Alfred nervously fingered the cloth under his trousers around his waist. "Those who see say his affair with the woman from Kuwadzana has only survived through the sheer Herculean strength of the medicine given him by his newly found *n'anga* in Mabvuku. But just as before, the dead woman will come and destroy his peace," the woman laughed carelessly.

"But why don't they all put their heads together and go to Masvingo to settle the case of this enraged woman once and for all?" the other woman asked.

"Go to Masvingo!" the plump one exclaimed. "The people there have made it very clear that they will only sit down with that family after they are given twenty five heads of them that move and moo. Where will our friends get them when they don't even have a fowl-run?" she spat on the ground viciously. "Their only reprieve lies with the *n'angas.*"

Suddenly, Alfred felt sick. Where was he coming from and where was he going? All he wanted now was to get away from the two women, especially the plump one with the careless laughter. How had he been thrown together with them anyway? Suddenly he turned and made to return to that damned place which all along he had thought was private. The two women stopped and stared back at him in bewilderment. What was wrong? They wondered.

At the gate, he met the landlord's son who told him that a man from Mabvuku had left moments before. Alfred walked on without paying attention to him and shut himself in his room. He stole a glance at the wardrobe mirror and a total stranger stared back at him. He looked closer, at the smouldering eyes, the squat nose, the neatly plaited hair, the dangling earrings and a smile hovered on her lips. Screaming, Alfred shot out of the room and shouting at the top of his voice, asked the son of the landlord in which direction the man from Mabvuku had gone.

A long time later, the sky was pale and dark and hard driving rain lashed the township, but Alfred kept running in painful circles, asking everyone he met whether they had seen the man from Mabvuku.

Men

"**M**en!" Mrs Furusa swore under breath. "Joramu!" she called shrilly.

"Yes, madam," the man answered.

"Come here," she said.

The man put away the dish towel that he was holding and muttered something to himself. He was tall and of big bulk and had a drooping, sorrowful face, prematurely greying eyebrows and sad eyes with dirty whites.

The man walked slowly from the kitchen into the lounge where the madam was reposing on the divan. He stood in front of her. Mrs Furusa shot him an angry look.

"Tell me, Joramu, why have I always to tell you not to forget to dust the furniture?" she asked, running her elegant finger over the handrests of the lounge suite. She swung her leg off the divan and sat up, revealing her thighs. Joramu looked away. "Do I have to repeat every day that this is pure oak and not mere imitation? Why must I complain to you every day that the carpet has not been properly cleaned? Do I also have to repeat to you that this is Persian? Tell me why?"

"But, madam, I . . . ,"

"But madam, but madam, every day. I am sick and tired of it. I want you to start re-cleaning the lounge immediately not only with the Hoover but also with dusters. I know you are doing nothing merely because I am not white. Are you hearing me?"

"Yes, madam."

"And another thing. I have decided to cut your full Sundays off by half a day. From now on you only have Sunday afternoons off. Don't look at me like that!"

Mrs Furusa stood up and walked off towards her bedroom. Joramu stared after her in silence, at her straight back and delicate stature. A wave of rage gripped him but just as quickly, ebbed away. Suddenly, he wished he was away in Rambanayi Beerhall gulping down mugs of Rufaro Super Draught with the deafening noise of drinkers all around him. Today was the last day of the month and if the madam was not pleased, he might not get paid. And already, it seemed the day had started on a sour note. He sighed.

"Joramu!" Mrs Furusa called from the bedroom.

"Madam!"

"Come here."

Joramu adjusted his white apron, muttered something to himself and walked slowly towards the bedroom. He stopped at the door and knocked.

"Come in!" the madam shrilled from inside.

The man entered. Mrs Furusa stood at the foot of the huge double bed.

"Tell me, Joramu, why must I always complain to you that my bed should be properly made? Do I have to remind

you over and over that the frame and the headboard have got golden linings? She began throwing the pillows onto the floor. "This is certainly not what I pay you for. Look at the duvet? All crumpled as if it was straight from a cow's mouth!"

"But, madam, I. . . "

"*But madam* is all that you seem able to say. I want the bed done properly immediately. Do you hear?" She pulled back the blankets and threw them on the floor. Joramu stared at her in silence, at her bent frail back and her delicate stature. A spasm of rage gripped him but just as quickly, passed away. The urge for beer entangled, almost suffocated him. Mrs Furusa continued tugging with the blankets and then as if she had all along been unaware of his presence, quickly raised her head and stared at him.

"For how long will you stand there staring at me?"
"Madam, I thought I . . ."
"Fantastic. There is no need to continue 'thoughting' now. Heavens, Joramu, do something!"

Joramu walked unsurely towards the bed and began making it whilst the madam threatened that if the bed was not properly made, she would find it difficult to justify why she ever paid him. As he tucked the blankets under the thick mattress, he saw the madam's smooth feet slide past as she walked out of the room. He quickly looked away. Today was the last day of the month and it appeared that she was not at all pleased. He felt the softness of the pillows and the duvet with his coarse hands. He felt the coziness of the mattress and that sharp sensation of thirst entangled him again.

"Joramu!" she called from the bathroom.
"Yes, madam."
"Here!"

The man lumbered to the bathroom, his khaki uniform swishing and stood by the door. The madam continued

mumbling inaudibly to herself. When at last she realized that he had arrived, she pointed an accusing finger at him.

"What is the meaning of this, Joramu? For how long shall I continue complaining about how you should wash my undergarments? Haven't I told you before that you should not soak them together with my husband's? Haven't I?"

"Yes, madam, but. . . "

"Jesus! Don't make it so difficult for me to pay you today. These black men! Whether educated or not they are all the same," she finished, angrily tossing her husband's pants into the tub.

The man felt a spasm of anger grip him and as quickly, pass away, leaving his throat parched and yearning for a sip of beer. He watched the madam empty the entire contents of the washing jug into the tub. He continued watching her as she tossed the jug aside and stormed out of the bathroom pushing him out of the way. His flared nostrils caught the smell of her expensive perfume lingering above that of the bathroom lavender. Dazedly he walked back into the bathroom and stared unseeingly into the tub. He tried to separate the madam's underpants from the husband's but all he could feel was the painful thirst in his throat and the impossible weight of the shattered day. He stood up to collect himself and felt again the emptiness and futility of everything. Very soon, evening would fall and he longed to spend it in Rambanayi Beerhall with Vaida amid the flickering glare of the smoke-stained neon lights, the deafening, blaring sound from the jukebox and the stale, moist floating haze of human sweat and smell.

He lifted a pair of the madam's smalls and scrutinized them, staring at the initials JF embroidered on the helm and wondered why her first name, Jane, should begin with the same letter as his. And then it occurred to him that even the madam's husband's name, Joseph, also

started with the same initial. He wondered whether this seemingly endless chain of coincidence was of any significance. And then the madam started shouting at him from the bedroom that she saw no possibility whatsoever of him getting paid that day. The man listened to the soft patter of her feet as she paced listlessly around the bedroom, in the silent pauses that fell between the shouting, but his thoughts were already entangled with the intoxicating overcrowdedness of Rambanayi. He started filling the jug with water but he knew it was hopeless; he was trapped.

Suddenly he felt a spasm of rage grip him so hard that he forgot to turn off the tap and water flowed all over the bathroom floor. He quickly took up a mop and dried the floor. Meanwhile, the madam continued pacing in the bedroom, mumbling to herself.

Mrs Furusa finally let him go for the day without his salary long after evening had fallen but before Mr Furusa had arrived. Suddenly, the man did not feel like going. He hung around in the kitchen and passage way, hoping that the husband would come and lend him some money. When at last he realized that this was wishful thinking, he left sulking. Then he began to wonder why he had ever thought that Mr Furusa would lend him some money. He wondered why he could ever have thought that Mr Furusa would come home at all. In all his two years as their domestic worker, he had only seen Mr Furusa on very rare Saturday afternoons. He had never talked with him and he could swear he had never seen or heard him talk with his wife. He did not know what sort of a man he was. Meanwhile, the madam paced restlessly in the lounge.

The man cursed the huge automatic gate as he left his workplace and the painful sensation gave him a savage satisfaction. Back inside the house, he could still see the silhouette of Mrs Furusa through the drawn curtains pacing up and down the lounge talking to herself.

He found Vaida waiting for him at the entrance of

Rambanayi Beerhall.

"You are late. Where have you been?" she asked angrily.

"I. . . I. . . ," he stammered.

"For a moment, I thought you had decided to by-pass me and go straight to your home. Today, I would have followed you there. What do you think I eat and pay rent with?"

"I. . . I. . . "

"Don't tell me you haven't been paid?" she swiftly turned and looked at him. A spasm of rage gripped him but just as suddenly ebbed away. "Anyway, even if you weren't paid, it doesn't matter. I am sitting at the corner over there with an uncle from Norton. You don't know this one," she quickly added. "I will borrow twenty dollars from him and you shall give me the money to give back to him as soon as you get your pay."

The man listened numbly, not hearing anything. All he wanted was beer.

They at last sat down and Vaida was given the twenty dollars by the uncle from Norton and Joramu began the long painful journey to reach himself.

They easily downed four two-litre mugs of super draught and Joramu, now that he had money, suggested that they switch over from draught to clear beer and he bought the four of them each a bottle. Again and again he bought beer, then, down to his last dollar, he borrowed more money from the uncle from Norton.

By the time the bar closed, the man owed the uncle from Norton a staggering forty dollars, just about a quarter of his entire monthly salary. As they stood outside the beerhall in the blinding glare of the township tower lights, Vaida suggested to him that since he had to go home to his wife and children, she would ask the uncle from Norton to see her home before proceeding to Kambuzuma where he was putting up for the night. Joramu bade them goodnight and trudged home alone.

He finally reached himself as he turned the familiar

corner to the place where he lodged. A spasm of rage gripped him and stayed. It began smouldering, eating his insides away like a cancerous growth. Somehow, he felt cheated, betrayed, without money and amazingly sober. He hated himself and almost succumbed to a wild urge to cross over at Mai Dadirayi's shebeen for just one beer on credit. But when he realized he already owed her over twenty dollars from his previous drunken sprees, he went home. And when he began to imagine what the uncle from wherever could be doing with Vaida, his smouldering anger nearly suffocated him.

He opened the creaking gate and walked past the main house to the small house behind, where he occupied two small rooms. His wife lit a candle and opened the door for him. He sat hunched on one corner of the ramshackle bed and asked for his food. His wife stood up and gave him the food.

"Tell me, Mai Rudo, what is the meaning of all this?" he exploded. "For how long will I continue complaining to you about cold food? Haven't I told before that I want my food hot?"

"There is no paraffin in the stove, Baba vaRudo." That spasm of anger flickered and his arms began to itch. "Why do I always have to remind you to do some of these small things?" he asked and without warning, slapped her viciously across the face. The woman cried out and fell on her back on the cold floor.

"There is no paraffin," she cried as he hit her again and again using his hands and boots.

The landlord heard her agonised screams and woke his wife but she only mumbled and swallowed. The landlord sighed, turned the other way and wondered whether he would get his rent that month.

An hour later in the small house behind the main house, Joramu paced listlessly up and down the small, suffocating room. His wife sobbed silently into the worn-out pillow.

"How many times must I tell you that I am the man of this house? And how long will it take you to understand that? I will repeat it over and over again for you today: I am the man of this house. I am the man of this house. I am the man of this house."

At last, the man sat at the corner of the ramshackle bed and said again and again that he was the man of the house until sleep overcame him. That night, he dreamt the madam, Mrs Furusa had been so happy with his work that she paid him double his usual monthly salary. And next to him on the ramshackle bed, his wife wearily wept into the worn-out pillow all night long.